THE ROGUE HEARTS SERIES

Unmasking The Duke

Donna Hatch

Mirror Lake Press, LLC
Copyright © October 2017

Other Works by Donna Hatch

The Rogue Hearts Regency Series:
The Stranger She Married, book 1
The Guise of a Gentleman, book 2
A Perfect Secret, book 3
The Suspect's Daughter, book 4

Courting the Countess
Courting the Country Miss

Heart Strings, Songs of the Heart series Book 1

Novellas and Short Stories
"When Ship Bells Ring"
"Constant Hearts"
"Emma's Dilemma"
"The Reluctant Bride"
"Troubled Hearts"
The Matchmaking Game

Christmas Novellas:
"A Winter's Knight"
"A Christmas Reunion"
"Mistletoe Magic"

Anthologies:
With Every Heartbeat, "The Reluctant Bride," Emma's Dilemma," "Constant Hearts"
Timeless Romance, Winter Collection "A Winter's Knight"
Timeless Regency Romance, Autumn Masquerade "Unmasking the Duke"
Timeless Regency Romance, Summer House Party "A Perfect Match"

Fantasy Novel: Queen in Exile

THE ROGUE HEARTS SERIES

Unmasking The Duke

Donna Hatch

Praise for Donna Hatch:

"Written with heart and depth, Donna Hatch's books are absolute must-reads for any fan of swoon-worthy historical romance." ~ Sarah M. Eden, USA Today best-selling historical romance author

"No one creates chemistry between Regency Historical characters better than Donna Hatch. If you want a "sweet" read, but with lots of sizzle, you have to read her books." ~ Author Carol A. Spradling

"Donna Hatch is one of the masters of clean romance with electric tension and smokin' hot kisses." ~ Reading is My Super Power Reviews

Interior Design by Heather Justesen
Edited by Heather B. Moore, Jennie Stevens, and Lisa Shepherd
Cover design by Lisa Messagee

Original Copyright: 2016 Mirror Press
Published by Mirror Press, LLC
ISBN-13: 978-1977705181
ISBN-10: 1977705189

Chapter One

Birthdays were overrated. People really ought to stop celebrating them after the age of sixteen. Snuggled into the featherbed of her sister's country estate, Hannah Palmer toyed with a croissant. This evening she might very well die of humiliation. Or worse, embarrass her sister and brother-in-law, the Earl and Countess of Tarrington, all in the name of birthdays. She let out a huff.

Alicia practically bounced into the room. "Happy birthday, Sis!"

Hannah smiled wryly. "I think you're happier about it than I am."

At odds with her rank as a countess, Alicia grinned and climbed into bed with Hannah and wrapped her arms around her. "I am happy about it. How often does a girl get to wish her favorite sister happy eighteenth birthday?"

Hannah gave her a wry smile. "I'm so relieved to learn I'm your favorite, since I have no competition."

Alicia laughed. "It would be sad if I claimed

another for that auspicious honor." She wound a strand of Hannah's blond hair around her finger.

"You're more energetic than usual today."

"Little Nicholas actually slept all night long." A maternal tenderness crept into Alicia's expression as it always did when she spoke of her infant son.

When the time came—if it came—Hannah planned to keep her baby in her room, rather than follow the convention of letting a nursemaid care for her child during the night hours. She vowed to be the devoted, loving mother her sister had already proved to be. Of course, Hannah might never realize the sweet dream of motherhood.

Alicia twisted around in bed and fixed her amber gaze on Hannah. "And I'm so happy that you're finally letting me throw a ball in your honor."

Hannah winced. "Yes, I just adore big parties filled with rooms of people I don't know."

"I know how you feel about it, dearest," Alicia said soothingly. "But this will be a good practice for you before you go to London this Season. When I'm finished with you, society will toast you as the New Incomparable."

"I'll be a clumsy, tongue-tied idiot, just like always."

"You're only clumsy when you're nervous. More practice at social events will help you not to be nervous."

2

Not be nervous in public? Hardly likely.

Alicia tapped her on the nose. "You are a beautiful and accomplished daughter of a respected gentleman, and the sister of a countess. No need to fear."

"I hear blonds aren't fashionable this year."

"The only ones who say blond hair isn't in fashion are those who are jealous. Just keep your head high and smile as if you know an embarrassing secret about everyone."

Hannah stared into the flames writhing in the hearth. "It's not that simple."

"It is that simple." Alicia squeezed her. "If you say next to nothing, everyone will think you are mysterious and will be all the more fascinated with you. Besides, you'll wear a mask tonight. Surely anonymity will lend you courage."

"I hope you're right."

Spending the evening alone with Alicia and her charming husband, Cole, would be preferable to a room full of strangers. But perhaps Alicia was right; a costume mask might help Hannah find some courage buried deep inside.

Hannah put a large spoonful of lumpy brown sugar into her chocolate, followed by a dash of cream. While Alicia rhapsodized about the ball, Hannah stirred absently before wrapping her hands around the china to warm her fingers.

Alicia ended on a sigh. "Maybe you'll meet *him* tonight."

"Him?" Hannah sipped the chocolate and snuggled into her pillows to drink the hot liquid turned decadent by the addition of the sugar and cream. Why most people chose to drink chocolate in its bitter form remained a mystery.

"Him," Alicia repeated. "The man of your dreams. Your future husband."

Hannah said dryly enough to be impertinent had she been speaking to a lady of rank who was not her sister, "Yes, meeting *him* at a ball would be convenient. I am persuaded that one must have a bit of cliché in one's life to obtain a measure of happiness."

"Only if you think marrying a wonderful man is cliché."

Chuckling, Hannah shook her head. "You know very well I speak of meeting at a ball." After setting aside her tray, she threw back the counterpane and stood. "I believe after breakfast, I'll go for a walk, perhaps pick some flowers.'

Alicia's brow furrowed. "Oh dear. Are you sure that's wise? I wouldn't want you to suffer from one of your sick headaches."

As she tied her dressing robe around her waist, Hannah exhaled a groan. "I'm not a fragile doll."

4

"No, but the sunlight does seem to bring on those dreadful headaches. And with your frail health, you ought to be careful."

It was all she could do not to snap at her sister. "My health isn't frail; I merely get occasional headaches."

Alicia gentled her voice. "Hannah, people don't normally get the kind of headaches where they must be shut up in a dark room with no noise for two days."

"Some do; the doctor has seen them in other patients. And I haven't been truly ill for years. Honestly, I'm tired of everyone treating me like an invalid."

"I'm sorry, dearest. I just don't want anything to interfere with your enjoyment tonight."

Hannah drew a long breath, releasing her agitation but not entirely pushing back her fear that she *was* sickly and might not be healthy enough to properly manage a household. Or more critical still, bear children. "I know."

She headed toward her dressing room but stumbled over something in her path. After sending a glare at the slippers that had tripped her, she shook her head. So much for only being clumsy when nervous. She must have missed the day the Almighty handed out gracefulness.

"There you are." Cole's voice boomed from the doorway.

Halting, Hannah wrapped her arms around herself and backed up slowly. Though Cole was her brother-in-law, a man in her room while she was in a state of *dishabille* pushed propriety. But she needn't have fretted; Cole's eyes focused solely on Alicia. Though he and her sister had been married almost three years, and Hannah had spent much time in his presence, such a powerful gentleman still sometimes left Hannah little better than speechless. Alicia hoped Hannah would meet someone like Cole in London, but the idea of hosting the type of guests a peer would entertain in his home left Hannah with the urge to hide—preferably in the library with a good book.

Surely she could find a country squire who sought little to no contact with society and all its games and demands, someone who would not require his wife to live in the center of the *beau monde*.

Of course, any husband would expect children, which might be problematic. Was she doomed to spinsterhood?

"I have an appointment with Suttenberg," Cole continued. "And then I am at your disposal for the rest of the day."

Hannah almost shuddered at the mention of an

even more powerful man than Cole. Conveniently, the Duke of Suttenberg didn't appear to know Hannah existed.

Alicia crossed the room and took Cole's hand, smiling as he kissed her fingertips. "Thank you. I want this ball to be perfect."

"You've certainly planned it to the most minute detail." Cole's eyes crinkled as he gazed adoringly at Alicia, the hard edges around him softening.

What would that be like, to be loved so deeply? All the men of Hannah's acquaintance treated her either as if she were invisible or incapable of original thought.

As the couple stood in Hannah's room, absorbed in their private conversation, Hannah strode into her dressing room, shut the door, and began her morning toilette of bathing and dressing with her maid's assistance. By the time she emerged, her room stood vacant, but the couple joined her for breakfast, happily discussing details of the evening, asking for her input on occasion.

Alicia's eyes sparkled and her cheeks flushed in clear delight. Hannah smiled at the sight of her sister so happy; she and Alicia had not always enjoyed such bliss. Through heartache of losing their parents and brother, and all the financial troubles that had dogged them afterwards, Alicia had taken care of

Hannah like a little mother. Alicia deserved to find happiness.

Alicia stood. "I'm going to spend a few minutes with Nicky before I check the progress of decorating the ballroom." She turned to Hannah. "Do you want to come? He's probably awake from his morning nap."

Hannah shook her head. "I'll visit the nursery this afternoon." Though she loved her tiny nephew, at the moment she couldn't bear to look at the sweet, torturous reminder of what she might never have of her own.

For now, she'd turn her energies to getting through the ball without embarrassing herself or her family. Later, she'd deal with a few of her other shortcomings.

After donning her favorite old pelisse and straw hat, Hannah picked up a basket and went to the renowned Tarrington Castle Gardens. The air smelled fresh and rich, and the golden morning shadows played hide-and-seek with the birds. The trees adorned themselves in the halcyon rust, burgundy, and amber they only wore for autumn's brief reign before their inevitable surrender to winter.

Hannah scoured the area for the last summer roses. Maids would surely fill her room with roses from the hothouse if she requested, but she wanted to rescue the garden-grown blossoms before the frost damaged them. Too bad the lilacs had already gone for the year. Carefully selecting blooms, she snipped them and laid them in her basket. Serenity enfolded her in its matronly embrace, and by the time she turned toward Tarrington Castle, peace filled her soul.

Surely she'd do well tonight. She'd practiced conversing with Alicia's friends, entertained a few gentlemen callers, and spent hours with the dance master. Moreover, she'd be wearing a mask so if she tripped or trod on someone's toe, no one would know her identity.

Humming and swinging the basket, she strolled along a path skirting the main drive while birds flitted and twittered and fat bees buzzed. Hoofbeats clattered up to the front steps. A sudden breeze gusted, and Hannah reached for her hat to ensure it remained pinned to her hair. The rider, wearing a multi-caped coat, dismounted by the front steps. He paused, tugged his clothing into place, and tossed the reins to a stable hand who trotted to him.

Barely giving the stable hand a glance, the rider said, "My visit will be brief."

The stable hand caught the reins and patted the lathering horse. "Yes, m'lord."

The visitor strode to the front steps. Hannah

wrinkled her nose. Though his hat concealed most of his hair and shadowed his face, only the Duke of Suttenberg possessed such arrogant mastery, as if he viewed himself ruler of all the earth instead of only his own properties.

Though she'd planned to enter through a side door, Hannah followed him up the front stairs so she could better observe the full force of his snobbery. And if she were honest, catching a glimpse of his handsome face would be no hardship. As long as he didn't turn his intimidating stare her way, she ought to manage to hold on to her wits.

He glanced over his shoulder. Her breath stilled. Though she'd spent time in his company four times—yes, she'd kept track—she was never fully prepared for his masculine allure. She'd seen plenty of gentlemen, including her brother-in-law, Cole. But the Duke of Suttenberg's face never failed to turn her to a blithering pool of mush.

The duke cast a passing glance over her and intoned, "Inform your master I am arrived."

Hannah's mouth dropped open, and her face burned with one part humiliation and two parts anger. He didn't remember her. Worse, he'd mistaken her for some house girl, a servant.

The butler opened the front door, drawing the duke's attention. "Ah, Your Grace. My lord is expecting you."

The duke entered without casting a second look at Hannah. Arrogant, thoughtless cad! That he would forget someone whom he should recognize by now spoke volumes to his conceit. Clearly, he viewed her as too far beneath his notice to have gone to all the trouble of remembering her face. True, she didn't like being the center of attention, but neither did she want to be treated as if she were a patch of mud to be scraped off one's boots.

As she ascended the steps, Cole's and the duke's voices boomed through the main hall as they greeted each other. She entered the main hall as Cole bowed.

"Your Grace. Thank you for coming. I would have gladly come to you."

The duke waved away Cole's words with a graceful motion of his hands. As they crossed the great hall toward Cole's study, the Duke of Suttenberg removed his hat, revealing a glorious head of hair that bordered on black, and peeled off his gloves before handing them to the butler following him. "'Tis of no consequence," he said grandly, probably thinking himself so magnanimous as to condescend to call upon a peer of lower rank.

"May I offer you a drink?" Cole offered. The study door closed, shutting off their conversation.

Hannah nodded her thanks to the head butler, who closed the door behind her, and handed her basket to a passing maid. Just to prove she was not as thoughtless as the duke, she looked the maid in the eye. "Would you see that these are put into a vase of water and taken to my room, please . . . Mary, is it?"

"There are two Marys employed 'ere so they call me Molly." The girl bobbed a curtsy and took the basket.

"Thank you, Molly."

A footman took her coat and hat and she thanked him. After firmly putting the arrogant duke out of her mind, Hannah busied herself with helping Alicia put the final touches on the ball. Noontime, as they sat at the breakfast table enjoying a cold lunch, Alicia glanced at the wall clock and worried her lip with her teeth.

"Are you worried the ballroom won't be ready in time?" Hannah asked.

"No, it's well in hand. I only wonder when Cole will return. He went to the fields with the duke and hasn't returned yet."

"They went to the fields?"

"Apparently, the duke discovered methods to improve crop yield and has offered to help Cole with our tenants'."

"Everyone seems to think the duke is some sort of expert on everything," Hannah grumbled.

Either Alicia failed to hear Hannah's ire or chose

12

not to comment on it. "He is wise beyond his years and always does everything exactly as he ought."

Hannah made a face. "A true paragon."

Alicia smiled. "I know you find him arrogant, but I'm sure he can't help himself. I imagine any child who inherits the richest and most powerful title and property, second only to a royal duke, would grow up to be a man become accustomed to . . ."

"All the bowing and scraping?"

"A high level of deference," Alicia corrected. "Everyone admires and tries to emulate him. He takes his duties very responsibly and has uncommonly exacting standards for himself, which is why he excels at everything."

Hannah sniffed. "And views the rest of us as insects beneath his boots."

Her sister laughed softly. "Very well. I can see I cannot extol his virtues enough to change your opinion."

"No, and it doesn't signify; Cole was born heir to an earldom and manages not to be an insufferable bore."

"True." Alicia stood. "I believe I'll lie down now for a few minutes before I return to check progress in the ballroom. I want to be well-rested tonight. You probably should nap, too."

Hannah glanced sharply at her. But her sister

seemed genuinely fatigued, so perhaps she meant the words sincerely rather than a prettily couched, overprotective statement about how Hannah ought to rest because "as we all know, you are rather delicate"—a statement that made Hannah fearful as a child, and frustrated as she grew.

Still, dancing until well after midnight would be fatiguing, not to mention keeping up with all the conversations and games that a large gathering required. Resigned, Hannah lay down until her lady's maid tiptoed in.

Hannah lifted her head. "I'm awake, Turner. What is it?"

"Beggin' yer pardon, miss but my lady wishes you to join her in her front parlor for tea. There are some gentlemen callers, the Buchanan twins and Mr. Hill."

Hannah groaned. "Oh no. What next? I was careful not to encourage their attention."

Turner gave her her a rueful smile. "Not enough, it seems, miss."

Hannah could dawdle long enough for the gentlemen callers to give up on her and leave. But no, Alicia was right; she needed to learn to overcome her shyness. Casting off the temptation to avoid the guests, Hannah arose. Over her shift, stays, and petticoat, she put on an afternoon gown of white muslin with blue flowers. After touching up her hair, she went to the main floor. As she headed to Alicia's back parlor, male voices and booted footsteps echoed behind her in the great hall.

"Ah, Hannah," Cole called out to her. "Is Alicia having tea in her parlor?"

Hannah turned. Cole and the duke approached, both walking as if they owned the world. Tongue-tied, Hannah nodded.

Cole quirked a brow at the duke. "Care to join us for tea?"

"Thank you, no. I must return." The duke passed a brief glance over Hannah.

Cole made a loose gesture. "You remember my wife's sister, Hannah Palmer, of course."

The duke blinked. "Yes, of course. Good afternoon." He might as well have said, "No, I'm sure we've never met"; it would have been truthful.

In a single graceful motion, he swept off his hat, revealing midnight hair and that distinctive patch of blond on the left side that apparently marked members of his family for generations. He appeared to be proud of the unusual birthmark judging by the way he parted his hair in the middle of it. Briefly, he dipped his chin in a ducal version of a bow when greeting someone of low consequence.

Seething at his arrogance, Hannah sank into a

very proper curtsy. In an act of uncommon boldness, fueled by ire, she offered a mischievous smile. "Delighted to see you again, Your Grace. I'm happy you've recovered from the strawberry incident." There. She'd made her point without revealing any hint of annoyance that he'd failed to remember her, and she'd even spoken without stammering.

His gray-green eyes opened wider, and his head jerked back ever so slightly in carefully controlled surprise. Was that a touch of blush on his finely chiseled cheekbones? Surely not. No one as perfect as the Duke of Suttenberg would do anything so boyish as blush.

"Strawberries. Yes. I'm careful not to give them the upper hand." His smooth baritone voice contained exactly the right amount of humor and arrogant *savoir faire*.

She might have been charmed by the almost chagrined smile now curving his beautifully formed lips if she weren't chewing on his admission that he refused to allow anyone, or anything, to best him. Not to mention that he still gave no hint of remembering her. He stood almost as tall as Cole, but where Cole had an intimidating breadth of shoulder, the duke had a lean, graceful build. But they stood with equally commanding postures inherent to peers who were lord of all they saw and knew it.

Saucily she tossed her head. "I wish you success in your endeavors to submit all strawberries to your whim."

Cole glanced at her in surprise, as if he couldn't imagine what had possessed her to speak so boldly. She could hardly believe it herself.

The duke's gaze flicked over her face, still showing no sign of recognition, but every sign of unconcern, although he did seem to study her more closely. "Yes, well, a pleasure to see you . . . again." He turned away from her dismissively and focused on Cole. "Until this evening, it seems, Tarrington."

Hannah marched to the parlor without waiting to hear Cole's reply. That duke! Insufferable, rude, arrogant . . . perfect people at the top of the social pyramid never seemed to have any tolerance for mere humans, nor would they do anything as lowering as willingly engage them in a true conversation.

Still in a pique, Hannah entered Alicia's parlor and tried not to glare at the trio of men who leaped to their feet at her arrival.

"Miss Palmer, how kind of you to join us," Mr. Hill called out before the twins could say a word. The young widower bowed low, revealing a thinning spot on the crown of his head.

"How lovely you look, Miss Palmer," one of the Buchanan twins exclaimed.

"Of course, you always look lovely, Miss Palmer," the other rushed to say.

They bobbed alternating bows while Hannah tried to sort out which twin was Edmund and which was Eustace. There. Edmund's face was slightly more angular and his chin pointed more than his brother's. Eustace's hair curled a little more over his ears. Both had barely reached their majority and probably had only started shaving a year or two ago.

"Gentlemen." Hannah gave what would loosely pass as a curtsy and sat next to her sister. At least this time she'd managed not to trip like she had the last time guests had paid a call.

The callers perched on the edge of their seats. Alicia drank her tea, smiling as if enjoying a private joke.

"I was just telling Lady Tarrington how much I'm looking forward to the masque tonight," Mr. Hill said. "I hope you'll do me the honor of saving me the supper dance." He offered her an awkward smile as if he the expression were unusual for him.

"I believe she is planning to save the supper dance for me," Edmund said.

Eustace cut in. "Surely you'd do me that honor, Miss Palmer."

From an assortment of pastries, Hannah selected an Eccles cake and bit into its buttery, crispy outside

18

to the current-filled inside. Though her usual shyness had faded with each encounter with the sweet boys, she still found it difficult to converse with people outside her family. Unless she was angry at an arrogant duke, that is.

Chewing gave her a moment to formulate a reply to the twins. "Since we are to be in masquerade, it is highly unlikely any of you will know me, nor I you."

"I would know you," Eustace said with an adoring smile. "I only need to look for hair the color of morning sunlight to find you."

She smiled at his poetic turn of phrase but shook her head. "What if I wear a wig?"

Eustace deflated.

"I'd still know you." Edmund puffed out his chest. "I'd recognize your figure and your walk."

Hannah cocked her head to one side. "I might be wearing clothing from a different era, which would alter the appearance of my figure." She took another bite of the rich pastry.

Edmund stubbornly shook his head. "I'll still know you. And I plan to ask you for two sets of dances. I wish it could be more." He eyed her hopefully.

Hannah smiled. That's all she needed—to dance more than two sets with one man in a single evening. People would think she was either "fast" or engaged to her partner. Of course, it was a masque; normal social rules did not apply. A liberating thought.

Next to her, Alicia shifted. "It sounds as if you all had better stand up with as many ladies as possible to be sure you have, indeed, danced with my sister."

"To be sure, I will dance with every lady present until I'm certain I've found you, Miss Palmer," Eustace said. "Well worth it."

Edmund looked thoughtful as if he might not recognize her despite a costume and mask. "I will, as well."

Mr. Hill took out his snuff box. "Gladly, I shall. I enjoy dancing and conversation as much as the next gentleman." His words, however, lacked convention and he shot an uneasy glance at the twins.

Hannah exchanged a knowing smile with her sister. Alicia had played that well. Now at least three gentlemen would dance with many partners in order to guarantee they'd found Hannah.

Mr. Hill carefully placed and sniffed his snuff. "I entertain a great deal, as you know. My late wife, God rest her soul, was a brilliant hostess. I'm sure you will be too, Miss Palmer."

Hannah held out her hands. "Ah, no. I prefer a quiet life."

"Nonsense," said Mr. Hill. "All pretty girls like you enjoy dinners and parties and balls."

Hannah stiffened. Mr. Hill had just proved how little he knew her with his silly generalization. She finished her pastry and sipped the last drop of her tea. She glanced at the gentlemen as she set her teacup on its saucer. She missed. It fell, landing with a thud on the carpet. Hannah cringed. At least the cup hadn't broken, and there was no tea to be spilled.

All three men leaped to their feet. Edmund got there first. Kneeling, he handed the cup to her.

"Thank you." Her face heated. Would she always be so clumsy in the company of others?

Then Edmund shot his brother a triumphant smile. Her embarrassment turned to annoyance. He didn't care to aid her; he only desired to beat out his brother for her favor. Were all gentlemen so competitive that they wanted to win, regardless of the prize?

And moreover, why did gentlemen either view her as a forgettable, possibly invisible, minor nuisance or a delicate flower without the strength to do anything more strenuous than lift a teacup? And heaven forbid she have likes and dislikes different from other so-called pretty girls her age.

Cole entered, greeted everyone, and went to Alicia. He kissed her offered cheek and sat next to her, devouring tea and scones as if he'd missed luncheon.

Eustace glanced at the clock and stood. "We don't wish to overstay our welcome, Lady Tarrington. Thank you for seeing us. Miss Palmer, I look forward to dancing with you tonight."

Edmund also stood. "Yes, thank you. I'm sure you'll be the loveliest two ladies at the ball."

Mr. Hill took the cue and got to his feet. All the guests said their good-byes, leaving Hannah alone with Alicia and Cole. Tension left her as quickly as the guests. If only she could skip tonight's masque.

Leaning back against the seat, Hannah folded her arms and addressed her brother-in-law. "Did you enjoy balls when you were a bachelor?"

Cole nodded thoughtfully. "I did back when I was young and green and eager to meet girls— especially because it took place when I had shore leave, and provided a nice diversion from the war, however brief. But balls and society games grew tiresome soon enough. Until I met your sister, of course." He put an arm around Alicia.

"The only time I stopped enjoying balls was when I had to hurry up and find a husband to save us from debtor's prison." Alicia cast a pained expression toward Cole.

Hannah nodded. "But that worked out all right, in the end."

"And so it will tonight," Alicia said. "It will be

magical. Just be yourself and let your costume lend you confidence."

If costumes could magically summon wit and grace and poise, tonight would be perfect.

Chapter Two

Bennett Arthur Partridge, the Fifteenth Duke of Suttenberg, bid farewell to the Earl of Tarrington, someone whom he would have called friend if he dared let down his guard enough to actually have friends, and rode to his brother's nearby home. As the afternoon sun waned, he arrived at his younger brother's prosperous manor house. A flock of children playing on the lawn scampered up to him.

"Uncle!" shouted his three-year-old nephew.

Grinning, Suttenberg dismounted and scooped up the child, swinging him into the air. Suttenberg groaned and staggered as if the child had suddenly grown too heavy to manage. "Good heavens," he teased. "Have you grown overnight? I do believe you are two stone heavier than yesterday!"

The lad squealed a laugh. "I big boy."

"Yes, I do believe you have promise of becoming a big boy someday."

"I big boy!"

"As you wish." Arguing with a child always proved pointless.

The other children danced around him, making

more noise than a gaggle of geese. His nephew wiggled to get down. Suttenberg chuckled at the happy cacophony around him. His nephew raced off with the other children, scattering a flock of chickens and splashing through an unsuspecting mud puddle.

"Be sure to get as dirty as possible!" Suttenberg called after them.

"I heard that," said a feminine voice.

Suttenberg grinned at his sister-in-law, Meredith, as she smiled at him through an open window in the parlor.

He strode in through the front door, handed his gloves, hat, and coat to the butler, and proceeded to the parlor where his grandmother, mother, and sister-in-law sat. Meredith bounced her baby, her second son, on her lap—the picture of maternal joy.

From where she sat on a settee, his mother, the Duchess of Suttenberg, looked up from a letter she held. Her lace cap set off dark hair and a pair of gray-green eyes exactly the color of his own.

"Good afternoon, Mother." He kissed her cheek tilted up to receive him.

"Is that my Bennett?" Grandmother called as if she were from across the room instead of in the next chair.

All attempts to encourage the dear old lady to call him by his title had, obviously, failed. Her use of his Christian name reduced him to a boy in danger of either getting a whipping or being drawn into her arms and kissed repeatedly. But it lent an intimacy that Your Grace and Suttenberg—titles that had replaced his name twenty-five years ago—never did. Those titles represented all he must do as a duke, including controlling the weakness in his bloodline. The name Bennett reminded him of who he was as a person inside.

"Yes, Mama, he's back," Suttenberg's mother, whom he still often thought of simply as *the duchess*, said. Smiling, she glanced at Suttenberg. "How was your visit with Tarrington?"

"Satisfying." Suttenberg took a seat next to her near the window. "We found a solution to his drainage problem, and he seemed pleased. He challenged me to a fencing match Tuesday next. Always a pleasant diversion."

He drew a contented breath. Helping a fellow peer solve a problem for what would probably become one of his most prosperous areas of farmland provided a satisfaction that serving in Parliament never quite provided. Oh, he did his duty, as always, but there was something truly meaningful about finding resolutions to complicated problems. Moreover, being the person with the answers, someone to whom others turned, added another layer to his present sense of pleasure.

The duchess indicated the letter in her hand. "Your sister has suffered yet another heartbreak."

"Oh dear," he murmured. Poor girl fell in love too quickly and never seemed to give her heart to the right fellow.

His mother's brow furrowed. "Apparently, he said he couldn't possibly live up to the Suttenberg standards, what with you as her brother."

Suttenberg paused, his contentment scattering like dry leaves in the wind. "Her favorite suitor dislikes the prospect of me as a brother-in-law?"

The duchess gave him a patently patient smile, as if he'd missed something painfully obvious. "He believes himself unworthy of you and the Suttenberg family reputation."

Suttenberg winced. "Am I so insufferable?"

"No, son, but you have a rather unimpeachable reputation, you know. Hard to measure up to that."

"Good heavens, Mother. That's doing it rather too brown. I'm simply trying to live up to the family honor, not frighten off my sister's suitors."

"It nearly frightened me away," Meredith said from her corner of the room. She shrugged apologetically. "I'm sure you can't help it that everyone looks to you as the standard in dress and behavior, and, well, everything. People naturally feel inferior in the face of such perfection."

Before Suttenberg could think of a reply to such a horrifyingly daunting and exaggerated statement, his grandmother cut in. "Did you find a wife yet, Bennett?" She looked in his direction, although her milky white eyes had gone blind years ago.

Suttenberg coughed. "No, Grandmama, I have not yet found a wife."

"A life?" She frowned. "I didn't ask about your life, boy; I asked about your wife!"

He chuckled. At thirty-two, he was hardly a boy. He replied more loudly, "I have not found a wife, Grandmama."

She thumped her cane on the floor. "Humph! You're dragging your feet, Bennett. Your brother already has two boys, and you aren't even married yet."

"Phillip was remarkably fortunate. It's not that simple for me. I have other—"

"Eh? Speak up."

He cleared his throat and enunciated, "It's not that simple."

"Pish." Grandmother waved her cane. "It's not so hard. Go find a suitable girl, and ask her father's permission."

He cast off all other possible retorts and settled with, "Yes, ma'am."

Smiling, the duchess nodded. "She's right, you

know. You should spend more time actually seeking a wife. Of course, that might prove difficult for a man of your station and reputation."

Suttenberg cringed. He'd only tried to step into his father's shoes, but instead he seemed to have created a reputation that even he would never be able to uphold. If people really knew him, knew the passions that heated his blood and were the source of a fierce temper, they wouldn't believe this so-called image.

Still, perhaps his mother and grandmother were right; he should actively seek a wife instead of relying on chance meetings at balls and dinner parties. But finding a lady strong enough to take on the responsibilities and social pressures of a duchess, not to mention someone whose family, background, and accomplishments fit his family's definition of "suitable," created a herculean task. It would be truly refreshing to find someone genuine, someone who might truly love him, hidden flaws and all.

He cast a sideways glance at his sister-in-law. His brother had been fortunate indeed to have found a lady whom he loved. But love shouldn't figure into Suttenberg's needs for a wife. The pressures of maintaining the image of superior accomplishments, which taxed him heavily, now expanded to the area of family and progeny, which raised the stakes. Sometimes the weight threatened to crush him.

"I invited Mr. Gregory to join us at your hunting lodge," his mother said. "I hope that meets with your approval."

Suttenberg nodded. "Of course. Gregory is always welcome, you know that."

His brother, Phillip, strode in. "Is tea ready? I'm starved." He kissed Meredith and rubbed the fuzz on his youngest son's head.

As if on cue, the head housekeeper entered with the tea service, followed by a maid carrying a second tray of scones, Devonshire cream, lemon curd, fruit, and cheese. The nurse took the baby from Meredith and carried him away so the young mother could more fully enjoy her tea.

"Is your costume for tonight's ball ready, Meredith?" the duchess asked.

"It is." Meredith's eyes glowed. "I'm going as Queen Eleanor of Aquitaine."

"Should I be worried you'll plot an uprising with my sons against me?" Phillip teased.

She cocked her head to one side mischievously. "Only if you become a tyrannical king."

They exchanged loving glances that seemed too intimate for tea. Or maybe Suttenberg's desire for such simple joy as theirs tainted his judgment. He looked away.

Very well. He'd seek a wife. It might help stave

off the brief moments of loneliness that had reared up lately. It would also have the additional advantage of getting his grandmother to stop harping on him to marry and produce an heir. While his family discussed the ball and their costumes, Suttenberg mulled over his newly realized goal.

How does one go about such an important task? Asking for his family's help was out of the question; they'd introduce him to a blinding array of ladies with practiced smiles designed to snare a peer. Chance meetings at balls and parties had only cemented his fears that most women were calculating and insincere. He couldn't exactly place an advertisement in the paper the way he'd found his secretary. His parents' marriage had been arranged. Phillip met Meredith by capsizing her boat outside Vauxhall Gardens—not, obviously, something Suttenberg would do intentionally.

Hmm. This wife-hunting business presented a problem. Cole Amesbury, the Earl of Tarrington, had a famously happy marriage. Perhaps he would be a helpful resource. All Suttenberg had to do was find a way of asking for his help while not appearing to do so. Giving advice to others came easier than asking.

If only he could find a lady with a kind heart and a healthy dose of wit, plus all the other requirements for a duchess, of course. It would be just too easy to find such a lady tonight while wearing a mask. His thoughts stuttered to a halt. Tonight presented a unique situation. No one would know he was the Duke of Suttenberg. He could be his true self. And maybe, just maybe, he could find a lady who would see him as a man, rather than the Duke of Suttenberg, and treat him accordingly.

But if she saw the real him, would the flaws he so carefully hid from others deny him such a pure love?

Chapter Three

In a mirror in the great hall, Hannah examined her Grecian-style white gown trimmed in gold—a lovely costume, but surely wouldn't save her from disaster.

Flowing fabric draped around her in soft folds and caressed her skin. A gold, multi-chained necklace lay heavily against her collarbones, the perfect finishing touch. The front of her hair, swept up into an elaborate braid piled on top of her head and woven with gold threads, appeared ready to topple, and the long curls down her back would probably go limp before the evening's end. And worse, she'd no doubt trip or step on her partner's toes, despite hours with her dance master. With her stomach so twisted up in nerves, she surely wouldn't manage to utter an intelligent sentence. Oh, why did she let Alicia talk her into this ball?

She pushed back her fears. Tonight she was Aphrodite, the confident, provocative goddess of love—above reproach. She touched the mask concealing the upper half of her face, drew a bracing breath, and entered the ballroom. Though secretly Alicia had thrown this ball in Hannah's honor as a birthday celebration, they'd chosen to make tonight a masquerade, so masks would stay on all night, unless guests chose to remove them for dinner. Hannah would leave hers firmly in place. Normally, Hannah would help Alicia and Cole greet their guests, but that would give away her identity, so she arrived in the ballroom like an invitee.

Fighting the urge to hang back, she stood with head high near the dance floor to watch the guests mingle. A man wearing the blue and silver tabard of a French Musketeer, complete with a plumed hat, stepped into her line of sight. His commanding bearing and the air of confidence enshrouded his lean form so completely that he might have been the prince Regent. In Hannah's limited experience with society, only Cole and the Duke of Suttenberg bore such wordless self-possession. All lords probably had such a stance. He stood perfectly still, his masked face turned toward the dance floor. Hannah followed his line of sight. Cole and Alicia, dressed as beautifully as a duke and duchess from the Elizabethan Era, complete with white wigs, took the floor as head couple. Other dancers lined up behind them. The Musketeer in front of Hannah appeared to search the crowd as if seeking someone. Perhaps the lady of his choice had revealed to him her costume and he desired to begin the evening with her.

The Musketeer's gaze made a wide circuit, turning her direction, and Hannah quickly looked away lest he catch her staring at him. She made a point of admiring the painting sweeping across the ceiling as if she'd never seen it. She was a goddess—confident and in control. She straightened her posture.

"My lady," the Musketeer said in a soft, husky voice.

She turned to him slowly, queenly, with all the confidence and poise of Aphrodite. "Sir?"

He extended a hand. "Would you do me the honor of standing up with me for the first dance?"

She inclined her head and placed her gloved hand in his. He led her to the line of dancers. Emboldened by her mask and the celestial attributes her costume lent her, she looked him in the face. Tall, lean, dark-haired, and with full lips, he arrested her gaze. Little else of his features were visible enough to reveal his identity to her, thanks to his costume, gold mask, and wide-brimmed hat. He returned her stare, but for once such focus did not leave her flustered and tongue-tied.

Cole and Alicia stood at the head of the line. The music began, an old-fashioned minuet. For a second,

Hannah faltered. Did she remember the steps? Lessons with her dance master seemed long ago, and they hadn't spent much time on dances from a bygone era.

As she curtsied, her mind raced. What came next? Her partner took her hand and led her without hesitation, his touch firm and sure. As she moved with him, following his lead and bowing again, her panic faded. She could do this. Down the line a lady's steps faltered. Hannah's heart went out to her. None of the dancers gave any indication they noticed the lady's misstep. Perhaps they all concentrated so hard on remembering such an outdated dance that no one noticed.

As the stately dance continued, her partner radiated supreme equanimity. There. He almost missed a step, but only the briefest tightening of his mouth betrayed the crack in his aplomb.

As he led her around in a little circle, she murmured, "I can't remember the last time I performed a minuet."

"It has been a while for me, as well," he admitted softly.

The sequence took them apart, and Hannah danced with the lady diagonal from her before the steps took her back to her partner. Next, she curtsied to the gentleman across from her and danced with him, counting the beat silently. As she returned to her partner, he again took her hand, leading her through the next portion, careful to keep the rapier at his side from getting in the way. She wondered if it were a real weapon or merely decorative.

He turned his head toward her. "I am trying to identify your costume. Are you a goddess?"

"I am."

"Which one?"

Uncharacteristically pert, thanks to her costume, no doubt, she tilted her head. "I believe I'll let you guess."

One corner of his mouth lifted. "A Greek or Roman goddess?"

"Greek."

He left her to the lady across from him, stepping in perfect time. When the steps brought him back to her side, they bowed and exchanged only the briefest glances before it was her turn to dance with the gentleman across from her. Clearly an older man, wearing the black-and-white domino of the previous century, he led her with ease through that portion of the sequence, no doubt comfortable with a minuet popular in his youth.

The ladies in their group of four began their promenade. One of them muttered, "Oh dear, oh dear," and waited to get her cues from the others.

Hannah tried to give clues as to what came next to help the lady, and her features relaxed as she fell into step.

The minuet came to a close. They completed the final steps and bowed. As Hannah straightened, she lifted her gaze to her partner, who stared directly at her.

"I have narrowed down who you are," he stated.

"You have?" Alarmed that he might already have determined her name, she barely controlled the rising fear that threatened to strip away all her false confidence.

"You aren't Athena or Artemis because you have nothing of a warrior about you."

Relief left her almost weak in the knees. She scolded herself. He was, of course, speaking of her costume's identity. "No, not Athena nor Artemis."

"And you don't have anything earthy about you, so you aren't Rhea or Demeter. You are beautiful and regal, so unless you are one of the lesser goddesses, I believe you are Ernos, the goddess of dawn, or Aphrodite, goddess of love and beauty, or evenHera, goddess of them all."

She studied him more closely, intrigued by his perceptiveness. "Which do you believe I am?"

As the dancers dispersed, he offered a hand again to lead her off the dance floor. "If I were to place a wager, it would be on Aphrodite."

"What if I remove my mask to reveal I'm not beautiful?"

He lowered his voice to a volume as to only be heard by her. "Of what I can see of you at this moment, you are beautiful. Your skin, what I can see of it, is flawless, and your lips are shaped like a rose bud. Yes, you are outwardly beautiful. I have no doubt."

Hannah's mouth fell open slightly. She'd never in her life been paid such a lovely compliment. It took putting on a mask to earn such a rare gift. Yet surely only a practiced flirt would say such a thing.

He added, "You are also inwardly beautiful—kind to your fellow dancers, you dance with uncommon grace, and comport yourself like a queen."

If ever she were to swoon over pretty words, this would be the right moment. Alicia was right; there were many practiced flirts in society. Hannah had best not fall for their flatteries. She inclined her head. "You are kind to say so, but I suspect you are a smooth-tongued rogue who goes about charming women everywhere."

"I assure you, madam, I spoke with perfect sincerity."

She might never learn the truth. The mystery of his identity and the meaning of his words sent a thrill racing down her spine. "Then I thank you. And I offer a compliment of my own: you dance beautifully. I am grateful to you for your skillful guidance."

"I am happy to be of service. May I bring you a drink? Lemonade?"

A gentleman dressed as a pirate, complete with a cutlass at his hip, appeared next to her. "Stand up with me, my lady, I beg you."

Hannah paused. That voice seemed familiar. Could it be Mr. Hill? Surely he hadn't discovered her so quickly.

The pirate grinned and swaggered. "Dance with me, or I might be forced to carry you off to my pirate ship."

The voice seemed like his, but she couldn't believe he'd say such a thing nor even grin at her thusly . . . unless the mask tapped into another side of him, as well. Still, it was only a dance. Surely no harm would come from that.

She carefully lowered her voice to alto tones to protect her identity. "Very well, sir pirate. But as we are a great deal inland, I doubt your ship is accessible this eve."

"I'm very resourceful."

She glanced back at the Musketeer. "Another time for the lemonade, sir?"

"As you wish, my goddess." He bowed grandly.

The pirate took her hand and led her to the dance floor. He leaned in too closely. "You look beautiful." The alcohol on his breath burned her eyes.

She glanced in his direction, trying not to inhale too deeply, and inclined her head. "You're kind to say so."

A quadrille began, and Hannah relaxed; not only did she know this dance well, but partners changed so frequently that there would be little time for conversation. Still, the pirate studied her carefully. She barely glanced at him. If she gave him little notice, he'd see she had no interest in getting better acquainted. The vigorous quadrilled proved an exhilarating diversion. She was breathless and light hearted by its end, until she returned to the pirate for the final turn.

As the next dance in the set began, he leaned in. "Hannah?"

She turned her head slowly. "Who?"

"I know it's you, Hannah."

Tempted to shrink from him, she raised her chin. "I hope this Hannah person is either your sister or your wife, sir, or she may not forgive you for using her Christian name."

He took a firm hold of her elbow. "I know it's you. I told you that I would know you even in costume."

She wrenched her arm out of his grasp and made a point of refusing to speak to him or look at him. Through the course of the cotillion as she changed partners, she danced with the musketeer. "We meet again, *Monsieur* Musketeer."

"Are you enjoying your visit among us mere mortals, Aphrodite?" His smile teased, warm and almost intimate without being threatening.

"Very much. I believe there are a few couples who may need my assistance falling in love, but others seem to be getting along famously without me."

He chuckled. "Have you chosen someone for me?"

"I am not a matchmaker, sir. I merely watch over and help lovers who have already found each other."

"Ah, unfortunate. Couldn't you make an exception for me?"

"Perhaps."

The sequence took them apart and returned them to their partners. At the end, they bowed and she lost sight of him.

The moment she returned to the pirate for the final bow, she said, "Thank you for the dance." Head high, she strode away from him.

To her relief, another gentlemen less interested in her identity asked her to dance the next set, and she lost sight of the pirate. As the evening wore on, her confidence increased. She hadn't missed a step and conversed easily with everyone she met. Perhaps a mask was all she needed to find her poise. She smiled the whole time, blissfully moving to the music and with other dancers. Who would have believed a secret identity would be so liberating? The pirate appeared across the room, but moved out of her line of sight.

After a lively country dance, Hannah took a moment to catch her breath, and the Musketeer found her again.

He smiled. "What must I do to win the favor of the goddess of love, that she might help me find a lady?"

"You pose an interesting problem, Sir Musketeer."

He stepped nearer, a bit more closely than strictly proper. "Am I a problem because you are tempted to match me with yourself?"

She smiled secretively. "Is that your wish?"

"At this moment, I wish that more than anything." The intensity of his eyes almost stripped away her carefully constructed ruse and touched the real woman inside.

In an attempt to put up her shields lest he cast some kind of spell over her, she tossed her head and laughed. "A lofty goal—to be loved by a goddess."

"To be loved by a good woman is a lofty goal, as well." He gently enfolded her hand in his. "What is your loftiest goal, Aphrodite?"

For a moment, she could hardly speak. His words touched a place deep in her heart. "I wish more than anything to be loved by a good man."

"Dance the supper dance with me; you can determine if I meet your definition of a good man." He smiled, his tone teasing as if still in the role of a swashbuckling Musketeer, but that intensity in his gaze suggested a deeper meaning. The warmth of his hand, even through their gloves, bathed her entire body.

The pirate appeared. He gave the Musketeer a brief once over, pointedly looking at their hands. Holding hands was intimate, bordering on scandalous. She withdrew from the Musketeer's touch. Even Aphrodite knew boundaries.

In a clear dismissal of the Musketeer, the pirate turned to Hannah. "The supper dance is next. Stand up with me." He grabbed her hand.

The Musketeer stiffened but remained silent, waiting for her to speak. Which was nice, really, since so many men seemed to speak for her.

She pulled out of his grasp. "I'm afraid I cannot. This gentleman has already asked for the supper dance."

"So sorry, good sir." The Musketeer held out his arm and waited for Hannah to take it.

The pirate gripped her elbow. "Why are you toying with me?"

More annoyed than alarmed, Hannah turned her head slowly to make eye contact with him and drew from a cool reserve inside her. "Release me."

The pirate looked down as if only now realizing he'd seized her.

"The lady asked you to release her." The Musketeer took a step closer to the pirate. "Do so this instant, or I shall be obliged to intervene."

The pirate let go of Hannah. With a sullen glance at the Musketeer, the pirate affected a bow and left, listing off to one side as he walked.

"Cur," the Musketeer muttered. "Has he been bothering you all night?"

"He keeps insisting he knows me. He's harmless." But her elbow burned where his fingers had dug into her skin.

"Shall I warn him away?"

"No, don't bother. I'm sure he won't try that again." Still, Mr. Hill had never been so rough before; he'd always treated her like glass. He might be emboldened by his costume, or by drink.

The Musketeer's gaze followed the pirate's back. "He deserves watching."

His protectiveness should have been endearing, but all her life, people had tried to manage her. It grew tiresome. Still, the Musketeer was right; Mr. Hill's behavior suggested he might not be as innocuous as she had believed.

The beginning notes of the supper dance began, and the Musketeer's mouth curved. "A waltz. Fortunately there are no patronesses who must be begged for permission."

Hannah returned his smile. "A goddess needs no mortal permission."

He grinned. "Of course not." He bowed with a flourish and held out his hand, waiting for her to extend hers.

The pirate had simply grabbed her, but this man waited for her to give her hand to him. She placed her hand into his and stepped into dance position with him. He led her with ease borne from practice and inherent skill. Instinctively she matched his subtle clues, and they moved together as if they'd been partners for years.

His voice wrapped around her with all the warmth of his touch. "There is something very different about you, Aphrodite. You are extremely self-possessed, and you stand apart from the others. It isn't arrogance or coyness; I can't pinpoint what it is about you that captures me."

How could she resist such beautiful words? It had to be the flattery of a *roué*, but it sounded sincere. Still, they were in costume. He clearly played a role just as she did. "I'm sure every mortal feels this way about a goddess."

"I'm beginning to believe you *are* a goddess. It's refreshing to have found a woman who doesn't want anything from me."

"Do women often want things from you?"

"Usually." His mouth pulled to the side in a mixture of bitterness and resignation.

"Does your Musketeer costume come with a name? I feel rather strange that I don't know what to call you."

"You may call me Bennett."

He smiled, and her insides took on the consistency of pudding. If she weren't careful, she would be in danger of losing her heart to this charming stranger.

Chapter Four

The goddess in Suttenberg's arms tilted her head to one side. "Bennett?"

An uncomfortable heat crawled up to his collar. Why in the world he'd told her to call him by his Christian name, he couldn't imagine. Not even his mother called him Bennett. Was this a sign of his ancestors' blood coming to haunt him?

"Is that your given Christian or your surname?"

He gave one of his signature mysterious smiles. "It is a name by which you may call me."

"Then I shall assume it is a family name, and not a given name, or people would be scandalized."

"You're a goddess; mortals' opinions shouldn't matter."

The smile she gave him in return suggested a host of secrets.

"Besides," he continued, "for all they know, we might be married."

"We might be married to other people." She turned a searching gaze on him, her golden-brown eyes leaving him mildly exposed. "You aren't, though, are you? Married?"

"No."

"Truly?" For the first time all evening, vulnerability crept into her tone.

So, the goddess of love wasn't quite as impenetrable as she'd led him to believe. That crack in her cool, regal perfection warmed him, gave him hope. Strange, but he'd never wondered if a woman desired him; it had always been a safe assumption that women wanted him for something—his money or his title or some sort of favor they wanted him to bestow. A few less virtuous women wanted him for more pleasurable, but less honorable reasons. All seemed to have their own agendas.

"I give you my word, I am not married." He'd never been so glad to utter those words.

Her expression took on an intensity he hadn't seen all evening. "I do not speak to *Monsieur* Bennett of the French Musketeers. I speak to *you,* the man behind the mask."

He gazed directly into her eyes. "I give you my word as a gentleman, I am not married." He paused, relishing the almost imperceptible relaxing of her shoulders that suggested she cared. "And you?"

She smiled and glanced away, suddenly demure. "No."

Demure. Odd, she hadn't exhibited that quality all evening, not even as she'd danced with other partners. Yes, he'd been watching her. Closely. To the point of almost ignoring his other partners. He hoped the casual observer would remain ignorant of his interest in the goddess.

Unlike other balls, when practically every eligible female and her mother stalked him in attempts to capture a duke, he hadn't caught her looking at him at all. He should have found a way to hide his identity years ago. Tonight none of his partners stalked him, a refreshing change, but none of them intrigued him like this Aphrodite. He'd danced with many ladies in mask, but she alone occupied his thoughts.

He led her through the steps, holding her closely. For the first time, he agreed that waltzing was, indeed, an extremely intimate dance. Who was the woman behind the mask? What were her secrets?

He peered at her. "If I cannot ask you any personal questions while you are in the persona of Aphrodite, how can I possibly get to know you—the real you?"

"You seem resourceful." Her head took on a pert angle.

He huffed his amusement at the polite thwarting that bordered on encouragement. "Very well. Tell me something about yourself that doesn't reveal your identity, but discloses an aspect of your true self."

She tilted her head elegantly to look into his eyes. "Today is my birthday."

"Is it?" Too bad he couldn't give her an appropriate gift. Or a birthday kiss.

"My favorite color used to be lavender, but after years of mourning, I now detest it. My new favorite color is pink."

Before he could express his condolences that she'd been in mourning, she pursed her lips into a tiny pout, so irresistible that he could hardly prevent himself from leaning in and kissing her. Right there. On the dance floor. In front of the entire assembly.

Her voice refocused his thoughts. "I detest blood pudding. I love the smell of lilacs. I put cream and sugar in my chocolate. I adore strawberries. I have never been outside of England, but I want very much to see all of the British Isles. And France. And maybe Germany someday—I've been studying German. And I like Shakespeare's comedies. I've read them all." She smiled. "Does that satisfy your curiosity?"

"It's a start."

Her mouth curved deeply, surpassing amusement and traveling into genuine, unrehearsed pleasure. How refreshing not to find a practiced smile. "And you?"

He thought back, trying to bring forward similar

personal details that wouldn't give away his identity. "I don't believe I have a favorite color, but I'm partial to both green and blue. I hate bread pudding. I love the smell of books. I put cream and sugar in my coffee. Eating strawberries makes my neck develop red marks and itch. I like Shakespeare's comedies, too, but I haven't read them all. I have a desire to see Italy, but I don't speak Italian. My mother's mother was German; she insisted I speak German when I conversed with her. I called her *Oma*. But after she died, I forgot most of the language."

Strange, but everyone of his acquaintance, including his family, probably had little to no knowledge of the trivial facts—except the strawberry reaction—that he'd revealed to this mystery woman.

She grew more fluid in his arms. "It's a pity you don't remember the German language. While it sounds harsh to our ears, it is imagery-rich and poetic." Her smile faded, and her golden-brown gaze fixed on him. "Do you think it improper for women to read and learn?"

"No, I applaud it. I enjoy reading and learning, and encourage others to do so."

Her smile was both relieved and delighted. How charming to find a woman who revealed her emotions instead of playing coy.

His gaze focused on her lips again, and the

desire to kiss her struck with more force than before. He'd certainly seen his share of attractive women, and he'd lost count of the number of them who had offered themselves to him—with various implied stipulations and prices, of course—but he couldn't remember the last time he'd suffered such acute desire. Artlessly elegant, mysteriously genuine, her contradictory traits fed his fascination.

The waltz ended, and his arms practically refused to release her. Still, he took himself in hand and stepped away before he carried her off to a dark corner to thoroughly kiss her. He couldn't do that. He refused to abandon his gentlemanly duty to satisfy a primal instinct that was quickly getting harder to control, probably thanks to his tainted bloodline.

As she stepped away, she smiled a genuine display of dazzling joy that nearly knocked him off his feet. "Thank you for the lovely dance. My dance master was not nearly so skilled."

He studied her more closely, searching for clues to her identity, her age. Though she followed his lead with more grace and skill than most, her comment made him wonder. Her mouth and the lower half of her face suggested youth, but with the upper part of her face and her eye area covered, he could only place her somewhere between sixteen and forty. "That was your first waltz since, wasn't it? You are newly out."

Again that mysterious smile. "My, you are getting personal. I don't mind telling you that I write with my left hand and that my hair color comes from my mother, but I won't give you any clues to my age. Besides, a goddess does not come out. If you must know, my dance master was the most skilled dancer who partnered me in the waltz, so I naturally compare all others to him."

A pertness touched the angle of her head, and she brushed lovely, long fingers over her gold necklace. The gesture drew attention to that hollow between her collarbone that his mouth ached to kiss.

She couldn't be more than thirty. Could she? No. Probably close to twenty. She said she wasn't married, but she could be a widow. That would explain her mourning comment. But it might be a parent or a sibling she mourned. Not knowing was about to drive him mad. Yet not knowing filled him with exhilaration.

He could be patient. He'd enjoy this guessing game until he took off her mask. And kissed her thoroughly. Not necessarily in that order.

He bowed low and offered his arm. "Dinner, I believe, my goddess."

She wound her arm around his, an innocent gesture he'd experienced hundreds of times, but tonight it became a sensual experience that sped the current of his blood into something more closely resembling a raging river after a storm. How could he eat in this condition?

With the intriguing lady at his side, he puffed out his chest as he led her to dinner. As liveried footmen brought dozens of dishes for the first course, he smirked and gestured to a nearby bowl. "I believe it's blood pudding. Shall I pass it to you?"

She grimaced. "I'll be sure to give you an extra helping of strawberries, sir."

He shivered exaggeratedly. "Greek mythology should have taught me never to anger a god, or in this case, a goddess."

"Anger, no, but tease gently? Perhaps. I suppose men cannot help themselves. My brother certainly took great delight in teasing me."

"Older or younger brother?"

Her smile dimmed. "Older."

Very gently, he asked, "The reason you wore mourning and then half mourning long enough to dislike lavender?"

She nodded and sipped her wine, not meeting his gaze.

"I'm very sorry."

She stirred her soup, staring into it as if her appetite had fled. "Thank you."

So, she had mourned a brother, not a husband.

The knowledge shouldn't relieve him so much. He changed the subject to bring back her smile. "You said you like the smell of lilacs; do you prefer them over roses?"

Her mouth curved upward a little. "For smell? Yes. For pure beauty? Hmm. Roses look and smell lovely, as do camellias, but lilacs have more character. And roses are given so often they've become cliché."

"Noted."

She smiled as if he'd passed some kind of test. "Do you believe ladies are too fragile to do anything more than lift a teacup?"

He blinked, trying to find a direction she might be headed. He finally settled with honesty. "No, I believe ladies, at least some ladies, have strength most men underappreciate. But if a gentleman is taking proper care of her, she shouldn't have to do anything strenuous. However, according to my mother, childbirth was assigned to women because the Almighty knew men weren't strong enough to handle it. She says men have no tolerance for pain and turn into great babies."

She laughed softly. "An interesting point of view."

"It's true. I cry real tears when I get a hangnail," he jested.

A full-bodied, husky laugh burst out of her. He stared, amazed at the rich, sultry sound. A few men nearby turned their heads. She pressed her lips together, shaking her head, and took another bite of soup.

"I like to go for long walks," she said. "Some people of my acquaintance feel I'm too delicate to get any exercize."

"Because you are so petite?"

"I was frequently ill as a child but I am seldom ill now. Still, everyone watches me as if I'll break. Sometimes I go for long walks when they think I'm napping. I feel alive when I walking outdoors."

"I enjoy walking, as well. I also love to ride."

Her expression clouded over. "I don't like to ride."

"No?"

"Horses frighten me—perhaps another reason I'm treated as if I'm made of glass."

Her confessions evoked a protective instinct inside. He pictured himself accompanying her on her rambles, listening to the husky sweetness of her voice, watching the sunlight glisten in her hair. Did she wear a wig or was that golden mass all that hers? She had said her hair color came from her mother, but was what he saw real? He studied the top of her head but could not be certain if it were genuine or an expertly crafted wig.

"I promise not to treat you as if you are made of glass." He looked into her soft brown eyes.

Hmm. Brown eyes and blond hair was an unusual combination. Still, his steward was colored thusly, so the possibility existed that she was a true blond. Had he met any blond, brown-eyed ladies recently?

The corners of her mouth lifted. "I would very much appreciate you treating me like a person and not a glass ornament."

They fell silent as the servants took away the first course and brought the second. He sifted through everything she'd told him, looking for clues as to her name. Clearly, he hadn't learned enough about her.

"You mentioned not liking horses; did you never learn to ride, then?"

She shook her head slightly. "I haven't tried in years. Every time I go near them I'm so nervous that the horses always get jittery."

"They can sense it."

"I doubt anything frightens you."

He paused. "Dark water. I dislike swimming in water so murky that I can't see the bottom. I have an irrational fear that a monster will swim up from the depths, grab me, and drag me under. Childish, isn't it?"

"No, not childish; it suggests a good imagination." She lowered her voice. "I can swim. My mother said it was an unladylike activity. When we went to the seashore, we used bathing machines, but sometimes my friends and I snuck out and swam freely. It was glorious."

He chuckled at the rebellious gleam in her eye. Would she trust him with such information if they were unmasked? Probably not. He'd certainly never told others much of what he had revealed to her. Was it their masks or something about her that encouraged him to disclose personal details? Perhaps it was that sense of home that enfolded him in its embrace in her presence.

He steered the conversation to other topics. He tossed out casual comments about national events, and her views on social reform, the poor, the roles of landowners, and other subjects he didn't normally discuss with ladies. She met him head on with thoughtful, intelligent replies. When she didn't have an answer, she simply stated that before she could comment, she'd have to do some more reading on the matter.

He quirked a brow. "Do you like the smell of books?"

"Love it. A library is always my favorite room in a house."

Convinced she was quite possibly the most perfect woman he'd ever met, he probed further, discovering a thoughtful, insightful lady who surprised him on every level. He was tempted to fall down on his knees and beg her that moment to marry him.

How quickly could he purchase a marriage license?

No, he couldn't spring such a life-changing question on her. She deserved to know him better. But surely she'd be pleased to marry the Duke of Suttenberg.

Wouldn't she? He'd never worried if a lady would accept his proposal as a duke, but now that he'd met one who didn't know of his title, he had to win her on his own merit. Was it enough? An uncharacteristic uncertainty edged into his confidence. This was his chance to learn if he, Bennett, the man, deserved the love of a woman like his Aphrodite.

"You're thinking very hard, Bennett."

His Christian name spoken in her voice sent a ripple of awareness over him. "I am."

"About?"

"I'm not ready to tell you just yet."

After dessert was served and consumed, without the appearance of a single strawberry, the guests left the table.

He escorted her, sorely reluctant to release her. "I suppose it would be terribly improper of me to ask you to dance a third time."

With her lips deliciously curved, she nodded. "I am the goddess of love, not the goddess of scandal."

"Very well. I'll resist."

As they headed toward the ballroom, some wild compulsion seized him, scattering all reason. He ducked into a nearby room, pulling her with him. She looked up at him with that mysterious smile and went unresisting with him.

She glanced around, her eyes lighting up. "The library."

"We're not here to read." He closed the door. The stillness of the room, with the noise of the guests muted on the other side of the door, fueled his impulses. He turned to her and placed his hand over hers where it rested on his arm. "I'm about to ask you a very mad, very improper question."

"Oh?"

"What is your Christian name?"

Again came that mysterious smile. "No names. Not until it's time to take off our masks."

He let out an exaggerated sigh. "Very well. Then I'll continue to call you Aphrodite. And I must apologize because I'm about to do something very rash with a lady whose name I don't know."

She went still.

He slid his hands up her arms to her shoulders and drew her toward him. He tried to move slowly, to give her time to protest or resist, but he honestly didn't know if he could stop himself even if she asked him to. With one hand moving from her shoulder to her back, and the other touching that sweet curve of her cheek, he leaned in and kissed her.

Her intake of breath broke the silence. For a heartbeat, he feared she'd deny him, reject him, until her mouth softened, grew pliant. Her lips' silky texture astonished him, and the contact sent a concussion through his body like a cannon blast. Clearly, it had been far too long since he'd properly kissed a woman. While most of his body heated to a level of incineration, something deep in his heart sighed as if finally reaching a long-sought refuge. A choked groan escaped him.

He kissed her over and over, each time adding to an inner well he didn't know had dried. Though she kissed sweetly and with some natural skill, following his lead the way she had on the dance floor, she clearly had little experience kissing. Her innocence could not be ignored. This was a lady whose pristine virtue he had trod upon, and she'd be ruined if they were caught.

Reason cut through his primal hunger, and he

forced himself to end the kiss. He held her soft body against him, trying to rein in his galloping heart. After pressing his lips to her brow, he pulled back and looked at her face.

Her mouth, moist and overly full from their kiss, curved at the corners, and her eyes remained closed. Then, like the strike of flint against steel that sparks flame, everything about her changed. She opened her eyes and stared at him as if he'd just insulted her.

And he had. He'd dishonored her, taken unfair advantage. And he wasn't truly sorry. Except for her expression.

He touched her cheeks softly, briefly, before holding his hands out to his sides in supplication. "Please. Please don't look at me like that. I swear to you, my intentions are honorable." He swept off his hat and mask.

She blinked, her brows drawing together as if she couldn't believe her eyes. Her gaze drifted up to that blond patch of hair that marked generations of dukes in his family. "You . . . you told me your name was Bennett. But you're . . ." She seemed to have trouble breathing. "You're the Duke of Suttenberg."

She knew him? Perhaps she only knew of him. "I am Suttenberg. And I meant no disrespect. Please, will you—"

Before he got out another word, her hand blurred

and a sharp pain exploded on his cheek. Stunned, he stared.

Her mouth spread into a scornful frown. "I am not a trollop, and I will not dally with you. Your Grace!" She threw his title at him like a curse, turned, and fled the room.

That was the first time in his life that anyone had ever dared slap the Duke of Suttenberg. And it hurt more than he ever imagined, in more places than his cheek.

Chapter Five

Hannah fled the library, still grappling with the horrible truth. Her charming Bennett was the arrogant Duke of Suttenberg. How could she have liked him? Trusted him? Usually, she was a better judge of character. Remaining silent and observing those around her normally revealed much about them. But no, she'd played the flirt, and now she must face the consequences.

At least no one had happened upon them when they'd been alone. Kissing. She let out a groan as frustration and self-recrimination battered her senses.

What had come over her? She'd behaved foolishly. With complete lack of sense. She might have been ruined. Might still be.

With the back of her hand, she wiped her mouth. No matter how hard she tried, she couldn't fully erase the sweet, exciting bliss that had consumed her when Bennett kissed her.

Clearly, her reaction only stemmed from having fallen prey to a philanderer. Odd, the Duke of Suttenberg didn't have that reputation. But a man who went about luring girls he'd just met into isolated rooms and kissing them had no concern for the reputations or hearts of his victims.

She marched so quickly that she had to hold up her skirts to keep them out of her way, heading to the main staircase, intent upon locking herself in her room. A voice caught her attention.

"Wait!"

She glanced back. With his Musketeer hat and mask in place once again, Bennett—the Duke of Suttenberg—strode toward her.

Going anywhere alone while he pursued her would invite another unwelcome encounter. She changed directions and practically ran to the ballroom, slipping in between guests and worming her way toward the center of the room. The candles burned low in the wall sconces and chandeliers, casting a flitting light over the room.

Voices slurred with too much drink mingled with husky whispers and laughter. Couples stood close, ladies gossiped, girls who were newly out giggled, gentlemen rocked back on their heels and eyed ladies. Footmen carrying trays of glasses wound through the guests. With so many eyes upon him, the oh-so-falsely-proper duke wouldn't accost her and create a public spectacle.

As she stood shielded by the crowd, she took

several breaths, each time regaining another scrap of her composure. Soon the night would be over. She could do this. She was Aphrodite, the confident goddess who cared little for mortals.

After squaring her shoulders, she lifted her head and impassively eyed the crowd. Nearby, Mrs. Potter, dressed as a swan, fanned herself, flirting with a slender man wearing a domino, whom Hannah was pretty sure was a Buchanan twin. There. She'd make a game of discovering the identities of the guests. Of course, she didn't know all the guests, having only come to stay with her sister a few times before she moved in with them this past summer. Still, she recognized several members of the local gentry. Each gave themselves away in little ways—body shape, posture, gestures, particular ticks or habits.

The final dance was announced. Another waltz. She let out a strangled groan, shutting down memories of the way Bennett had led her—firm, yet gentle—in a dance that seemed invented for those few glorious moments she'd spent in his arms when she'd believed he was perfect, before he'd revealed his true character.

Mr. Hill, the pirate, turned his head in her direction. He straightened, clearly spotting her. With a growl of annoyance, she moved away from him. She didn't have the patience to deal with him right now.

He pushed through to her. "Wait," he said as he caught up to her. "Dance with me." He stepped closer, too close. His breath reeked of liquor, and he swayed on his feet.

Curtly, she replied. "No, thank you. I'm finished dancing for the evening."

He frowned but rallied. "It's too warm in here. Shall we catch our breath outside on the terrace?"

Why did men always think women wanted to be alone with them? If he thought she'd go anywhere with a man who was three sheets to the wind, he didn't know her very well.

"No, thank you."

"Then let's find a place to sit. The sitting room behoind that door?" He pointed to a nearby door.

"No, that would be unwise."

"Then—"

She held up her hand. "Sir, I have no desire to wound your feelings, but I do not wish to go anywhere with you. Not ever."

He swayed first toward then away from her, as if he stood on the deck of a ship. "But I adore you. I desire you. I—"

"Please, don't. It's best that we do not continue our association. Good evening, sir." She bobbed a faint curtsy and started to leave, but he grabbed her upper arm.

His mouth twisted. "Because I'm not the brother of an earl? Is that it? I'm too common?"

Her face heated as anger simmered her blood. "Are you calling me a snob?"

"You think you're too good for me, you with your lovely dowry and noble connections, now that your sister has nabbed herself an earl. But you're nothing but an upstart little social climber."

A third voice cut in. "Apologize to the lady this instant, cur."

Bennett stood next to her, his hand on the hilt of his rapier. But he wasn't her Bennett; he was the rude Duke of Suttenberg. Annoyance that he'd once again intruded into her life fueled the growing realization that no man believed her capable of lifting a finger for herself and heated the simmer in her blood to a boil. Suttenberg was just as bad as Mr. Hill. She wanted to throw something at the both of them.

Before she could speak, Mr. Hill snarled, "This conversation does not concern you, boy."

"It does concern me, so leave her be." The duke's voice, unclouded by drink, and his form, so tall and straight, formed a sharp contrast to the drunk man. Not that she wanted his interference.

Mr. Hill's gaze darted from the duke to Hannah, and he sneered. He turned as if to leave. Over his shoulder he cast one last barb, "That proud little doxy isn't worth it."

With a quick backward step and a metallic scrape, the duke stood in *en garde* position with his rapier gleaming in his hand, the point touching the base of Mr. Hill's neck.

A few nearby guests let out gasps of horror and delight at the sensational development. Hannah stared in open-mouthed shock. He'd actually drawn a weapon at a ball. Unbelievable.

"Apologize to the lady this instant, or I will not hesitate to draw your blood." The duke's voice, barely audible, cut through the din in the room.

Mr. Hill seemed to snap. Perhaps the abundance of alcohol, or his stung pride, drove him to recklessness, but he pulled out his cutlass, albeit more slowly than his sober opponent, and crossed his curved sword against the rapier's narrow blade. "I'll teach you to interfere with me, boy!"

Stunned, Hannah gasped, "No."

Mr. Hill lunged forward and swung his sword. The Duke of Suttenberg's blade bent under the weight of the blow. With a quick flick of his wrist, he disarmed Mr. Hill. The cutlass clattered as it hit the floor. Mr. Hill staggered back, swaying drunkenly, and nearly fell.

Cole appeared, his expression grim, and hauled Mr. Hill to his feet. Then, turning to the staring crowd, Cole smiled brightly. "Well done! Very entertaining! That's the best end to a ball I've ever seen!" He applauded as if the brief fight had been planned to amuse the guests.

Next to him, Alicia also clapped. "Bravo!"

Hannah joined in, admiring her brother-in-law's quick thinking. Apparently, the guests closest to the fight believed Cole's ruse. Their faces relaxed, and they took up the applause. Mr. Hill looked around as if he were in a daze.

While the assembly applauded the "show," Cole shook Suttenberg's hand. "That was a very realistic performance, Sir Musketeer. Thank you."

The duke put away his rapier and made a low, flourishing bow to the assembly. Cole patted Mr. Hill's back and led him away, still congratulating him on his acting skills.

Suttenberg turned to Hannah and opened his mouth, but she held up a hand to stop him. "Don't."

Nothing he could say would excuse his behavior. First the kiss, then the spectacle he created. The duke had fooled society into believing he was the perfect Englishman, but he was a discreet womanizer with little sense of propriety.

Turning away, Hannah touched her mask to assure herself it remained securely in place and pushed through the dispersing crowd. She'd had enough of tonight's ball. How could he have humiliated her that way? True, Mr. Hill's words had been nothing short of unforgivable, but they were only words. Suttenberg had actually drawn a weapon. If anyone knew what had really transpired, Hannah would be the source of gossip for months. Alicia's grand plans to launch Hannah into London society next Season would be tainted by tonight's altercation. With luck, tonight's guests would remain ignorance of the truth.

Hannah ducked into the servants' stairway. Taking the main staircase would reveal to Suttenberg that she was a guest of Cole and Alicia's. If she had her way, he'd never know who he'd shamed, first by kissing her, then by drawing a weapon over her.

She seemed to be doing a lot of hoping that nothing about tonight would be linked to her. Fate was seldom that kind.

Lifting her skirts, she practically ran up the back stairs toward the family wing, dashing past a startled maid who flattened herself against the wall and stared at the intruder in the servants' domain.

Safe in her room, Hannah rang for her maid and stripped off her costume jewelry. In the mirror, her flushed face stared back, surrounded by a halo of disheveled, limp curls. Outside her window, a clattering of carriages and hoofbeats kept up a steady rhythm as guests departed. Not that it mattered. Even if the ball weren't over, Hannah would not have gone back out there for all the tea in China.

Alicia burst in. "What happened?"

Hannah bit her lip as hot tears blurred her vision. "It was so humiliating. I can't believe it."

"Who were they? Was the Musketeer the Duke of Suttenberg."

Hannah nodded. Though tempted to keep it all secret, she'd never hidden anything from her sister. "The pirate was Mr. Hill. He'd had too much to drink and became a bit aggressive. He—" She swallowed and turned away, too embarrassed by what had occurred.

"What did he do? Did he touch you?" Alicia's voice rose in alarm.

"No. But he called me a social climber and a . . . a doxy."

Alicia gasped. "That scoundrel. He will never be welcome in this house again. I vow I will publicly snub him."

"Please don't. I don't want anyone to know or even suspect their fight was real, nor that I was the center of it."

Calming, Alicia shook her head. "No, of course you don't. What happened then?"

"The duke pulled out his rapier and demanded Mr. Hill apologize. You know the rest." She sank down onto the chair by her dressing table.

"His Grace is the absolute model of gentlemanly behavior. That he defended you comes as no surprise. But I cannot account as to why he'd draw a weapon at a social gathering. It's so unlike him."

"Yes, well, he isn't the model gentleman you think he is."

Alicia let out a long breath and actually smiled. "It was noble of him to rise to your defense. Still, if it weren't for Cole's quick thinking, the situation could have gotten out of hand."

"I hope everyone really did believe it was staged." Hannah hugged herself, still smarting over the duke's forward behavior in the sitting room. Did he truly think because he was a duke that every girl would abandon her virtue for him?

Alicia pulled off her white wig and smoothed her hair. "The guests were still bubbling over about the realistic display as they said good-bye, and even congratulating me on having such entertaining floor show. No one seemed to think the lady in the goddess costume had any part of the show."

"Good." Too bad the sword fight wasn't the only thing to have gone amiss.

How could she have been so foolish as to have allowed a man she'd met only that evening to kiss her? He probably thought her fast. Maybe she was. That kiss had been the most supremely perfect moment of her entire life. She'd never experienced such lovely pleasure, nor such astonishing sense of belonging.

At least she'd had the presence of mind to slap him. That should dispel any presumption that she could be coaxed into behaving like a hoyden again.

"You're still overset, dearest." Alicia knelt in front of her and drew her into an embrace.

Her sister's comforting touch and the strong emotions she'd experienced all evening collided. A sob wrenched its way out of her.

Alicia pulled away and looked at her. "Hannah, dear, what is it? Did something else happen?" She smoothed a stray strand back from Hannah's face, her touch affectionate, motherly.

The entire story came pouring out of Hannah— their banter, her bliss, her joy, the kiss, her heartbreak that the kiss meant so little to him, his attempt to use his rank to justify his taking advantage.

Alicia listened without judgment. When Hannah finished talking, Alicia hugged her again. "Going with him alone into a room wasn't the wisest course of action, but after what transpired between you two, I can't say I blame you. And you're right, a man like His Grace should have known better. Frankly, I'm shocked he'd treat a lady in such a way. Don't worry any more about it, dearest. If you never want to see him again, I'll make sure of it."

"I don't." For the moment, she was content to let her sister take care of her.

"Then you shan't. He's probably figured out who you are by now, but duke or no duke, he cannot make you see him. If he calls upon you, we'll turn him away. It's as simple as that."

Hannah let out an exhale, releasing her tension, and leaned against her sister, basking in her affection and the sense of order she exuded. All would be well. Hannah had survived her ball without tripping or getting tongue-tied, thanks to her false confidence due to her costume, and hadn't brought public embarrassment to Alicia and Cole. How she'd ever survive London, she couldn't say. But the Season was months away. Maybe by then she would develop some poise and grace without the aid of a mask. And she'd certainly avoid going into a room alone with a man ever again.

As she went to bed, the memory of Bennett's arms around her, his mouth kissing her so tenderly, crept over her. If only it had been real. Having tasted such sweet pleasure made her long for more. The next time she kissed a man, she'd be sure his intentions were more honorable than the duke's.

Chapter Six

Still wearing his Musketeer costume, Suttenberg stood in the study of Tarrington Castle, awaiting the arrival of Cole Amesbury, the Earl of Tarrington. No doubt, after the earl finished seeing his guests out, he'd return and demand an explanation. Or satisfaction. Suttenberg paced to the windows.

If Tarrington called him out, what would he do? He respected, even liked, the earl. He couldn't fight him. Would an apology suffice? Drawing a weapon at a party was a serious offense. But then, so was kissing a lady he'd only just met. He couldn't believe he'd done either. Had he completely gone mad? Perhaps his maternal grandfather's Italian blood had finally taken over as he'd always feared it would.

He ran his hand over his face, the memory of well-deserved slap burning his skin as if she'd delivered it moments ago. He paced back toward the other side of the room. He'd always prided himself on doing everything exceptionally well, on exceeding societal expectations. He served faithfully in Parliament, did his best to care for his properties and tenants, achieved a fearsome reputation for fencing and fisticuffs, avoided gambling and excessive drinking, and never trifled with ladies' hearts or their virtue. But tonight he'd broken every social and personal rule. Worse, he'd lost his Aphrodite.

Tarrington entered, eyeing Suttenberg as if he'd never seen him. "What were you drinking tonight?"

Suttenberg let out his breath. "I don't even have that as an excuse."

Tarrington sat and laced his fingers together. "Well, at least now I know you're human. For years I wasn't so sure." His lips quirked.

Suttenberg blinked. "I apologize for my conduct."

The earl waved him off. "The guests think it was an act."

"Thanks to your quick thinking."

Tarrington inclined his head. "My wife considers the evening a success. Everyone will talk about it for weeks."

"Still, I cannot excuse my temper."

"What happened? Did he insult you?"

"He insulted a lady."

Tarrington nodded sagely. "I have risen to the defense of many a lady, once to the point of dueling." Frowning, he stared down at his hands.

Suttenberg didn't pry. "It would have been

better form to challenge him rather than draw a weapon."

"No need to flog yourself—no harm done."

"You truly aren't angry?"

The earl grinned. "Angry? Are you kidding? Even if no one else knows it, I had the singular experience of witnessing the mighty Duke of Suttenberg in a rare moment of weakness. It may never happen again, so I'm relishing in it." Chuckling, Tarrington got up and clapped a hand on Suttenberg's back. "No one got hurt. No one became truly alarmed. The matter is closed."

The muscles in Suttenberg's shoulders loosened. At least he hadn't offended Tarrington, and he didn't have to face the prospect of a duel. Yet the earl's words offered little comfort. Suttenberg had behaved badly toward his goddess. He had to find her and beg her forgiveness. And convince her to give him another chance.

Tarrington interrupted his thoughts. "Is there something you wish to discuss?"

Suttenberg looked up.

The earl watched him carefully. "Unburden yourself, duke."

Perhaps he'd gotten into a habit this eve of speaking frankly. "You wouldn't happen to know the identity of a young woman dressed as a Greek goddess, would you? She had long, blond curls. That might have been a wig, I suppose, but it looked genuine."

Tarrington cocked his head. "Shy?"

"No, she was very poised and confident. Even a bit flirtatious."

"Hmm. I saw more than one goddess. My wife's sister is blond, and she was dressed as a goddess, I believe. But she is painfully shy, especially at large gatherings. I can't imagine her flirting."

"Your wife's sister? Miss Palmer, isn't it?"

"That's her. You've met her a few times, I believe."

A few times? He vaguely remembered a very young lady barely out of the schoolroom this morning. He nodded. "I don't believe she could be my Aphrodite." He let out a long breath. "Would you ask the countess? I must find her."

"Your Aphrodite? Ohhhhh…..a lady caught your eye, eh?" A brow raised, and the earl's mouth quirked to one side. "I don't recall you showing preference for a lady before."

"No, 'tis true. But this one was different."

"And she gave you no clue as to her name?"

"None. And then I made a fool of myself and kissed her."

Tarrington choked. "You kissed her?"

Suttenberg put his head into his hands, surprised that he'd confided in Tarrington, and relived the shame all over again. "Truly there must be something wrong with me. I don't blame her for slapping me. By the time I caught up to her, the pirate was talking to her. Apparently she spurned him, and then he grew insulting. And I snapped." He raised his head, expecting a condemning stare.

Tarrington's expression was a mixture of disbelief and amusement. "I'd like to meet the girl brave enough to slap the Duke of Suttenberg. Of course, you were in costume, so . . ."

"Ah, no. I removed my mask after I kissed her. She knew my face and called me by name before she slapped me."

"You do have a problem."

"I have several, in fact. I must come to terms with my own behavior. I must find a girl whose name and face I do not know, and I must convince her to give me another chance."

Tarrington nodded. "I'd only known my wife a few moments before I became equally obsessed."

Footsteps neared, and the door flew open. The Countess of Tarrington burst in, eyes snapping and chest heaving. The men leaped to their feet as the countess marched up to Suttenberg, wearing an expression of outrage.

"You kissed her?" she demanded.

Taken aback, Suttenberg could only nod.

"You scoundrel!" She raised her hand, and for the second time in his life—both in the same night—a lady slapped the Duke of Suttenberg.

Chapter Seven

Sitting in Alicia's sun-drenched parlor, Hannah glanced at the clock and sipped her tea while Alicia played hostess to her neighbor, Mrs. Potter. They rhapsodized about the triumphant ball two nights past, and all the delights of the evening, sprinkled liberally with speculations on who had worn what costume and who had been seen in whose arms.

At this, Mrs. Potter stopped and glanced at Hannah as if remembering her presence, before she returned her attention to Alicia. "Well, you know what I mean, of course, Countess."

Hannah nearly rolled her eyes. Just because she was newly out didn't mean she knew nothing about the foibles and passions of men and women. And after the ball, she had a better understanding.

Mrs. Potter smiled at Hannah. "And how are you, my dear? You didn't overtax yourself?"

"No, ma'am. I am quite well."

"I do worry about you. When you had to leave my dinner party a fortnight ago with a sick headache, I really was quite concerned. Young ladies with delicate constitutions cannot be too careful."

Hannah's hackles rose at the insinuation that she was so sickly neighbors must worry for her. She tried to sound gracious. "I'm quite well. Thank you for your concern."

"You know, my great aunt suffered from the sick headache, and she found it helpful to use leeches once a month. You might try that."

Nearly choking on her tea, Hannah gasped. "Oh, er, thank you. I'll keep that in mind."

"And don't exercise too much. My aunt simply couldn't tolerate going for walks. The exercise and sunlight always brought on a bad spell." Mrs. Potter tutted. "She never had children, poor dear."

Hannah's stomach dropped at yet another reason to fear she'd never know the joys of motherhood.

Alicia broke in. "I always keep careful watch over my sister."

Mrs. Potter said hurriedly, as if she feared she'd somehow offended her hostess, "Oh, yes, I'm sure you do, my lady. I'm sure you do. Well, I must be off."

After they bade farewell, Hannah let out a sigh of relief. Just to be contrary, she turned to her sister. "I'm going for a walk. A long one."

Before Alicia could reply, Hannah went to her room and changed into a sturdy pair of walking boots and took up a wide-brimmed hat. She carefully wove a hatpin into her hair to keep it in place. After donning a spencer against autumn's chill, she went outside. Meandering through the gardens didn't satisfy today; a good ramble through the country called to her. Forgoing the driveway, she took a circuitous route past the gardens out toward the river leading to the lake. The river, slow-moving and sluggish, gurgled in the autumn stillness. A songbird trilled overhead. She strolled along the river, following it toward the lake, passing the bridge over which the driveway crossed.

After a bend in the river, she came upon the lake. It spread out before her in shimmers turned golden in the afternoon light. Swans floated on the surface, leaving V-shaped wakes. Wild geese crossed the sky against the azure backdrop. She skirted the lake's edge as waves lapped against the shore. The solitude filled her with peace. Clean, earthy scents mingled with heather, freshly mown grass, and hay. Shadows grew long and a chill bit the air reminded her of the hour. If she stayed much longer she'd be late for dinner. Reluctantly, she turned back and followed the river toward the castle.

As she stepped over the path strewn with rocks and blanketed with a damp carpet of leaves, her foot slipped. She sat down hard. Pain splintered up her leg.

"Oh bother!" Her clumsiness usually originated from nervousness in the presence of others, but she certainly had her share of ungraceful moments in private, as well.

Sitting awkwardly on the damp ground, she righted her legs. She tried to climb to her feet, but pain in her ankle stopped her. She paused, resting, and tried again to put weight on that foot. This time the pain lessened. Perhaps she could walk out the soreness. At least she hadn't fallen in the water, which would be more her usual style.

She took a few more paces. Her ankle throbbed worse with each step. She found a boulder and sat, careful to keep her ankle straight. The river's song filled her ears, and she watched it ripple toward the lake, momentarily forgetting her discomfort and her desire to return home. Gold and red leaves fluttered from overhead to land on the surface and ride the current like tiny boats. The shadows grew long, and the temperature cooled. Alicia would worry if Hannah didn't return home soon.

Hannah stood and continued. Each step sent waves of pain up her leg. At least she could walk, if a bit slowly. If she followed the driveway, she'd have the smoothest path and the shortest distance back to Tarrington Castle. After only moments, she reached the driveway.

A horse's hoofbeats approached from behind. A lone rider astride an enormous stallion cantered around the bend in the narrow driveway. He rode beautifully, like one born for the saddle. Hannah moved to the side of the road to allow the rider plenty of room to pass without bringing the frightening animal too close.

The rider slowed to walk next to her. "Are you in need of assistance, miss?"

The Duke of Suttenberg's smooth voice drew her gaze. He sat astride, looking at her like she was some kind of waif. Her cheeks heated. Not him. Not the duke who'd kissed her like she was some kind of tart.

With any luck, he'd go away and take his big, scary horse with him. "No, thank you."

He leaned in as if to peer at her around her hat. "You look familiar. Have we met?"

What a question! She lowered her head to use the brim as a shield. However, he never seemed to remember her the other times they had been introduced, so the odds of him knowing her face or name now seemed unlikely. At least he didn't mistake her for a servant today. Just a waif. Oh, that was so much better!

"I don't think so." She flushed at the lie. But telling him any different would be pointless. As often as they'd been introduced, how he never seemed to remember her was a mystery. Either he had the worst memory of any person alive, or she was truly forgettable—to all but the Buchanan twins and Mr. Hill.

Go away, go away, go away, she silently chanted. She couldn't bear it if he discovered her to be the hussy who had dressed and acted like Aphrodite and brazenly kissed strangers. And liked it. But despised herself for liking it.

"You're limping. Have you injured your foot?"

"I'm perfectly well. No need to worry. Continue on." She made a point of walking on her fiery, throbbing foot as evenly as possible.

He stopped his horse. Just as she began to believe he would leave, the creaking of leather drew her attention again. With practiced grace, he dismounted and walked next to her, leading his horse by the reins. Good heavens, the beast was huge! But at least the tall man next to her walked between her and the animal. He appeared to have control over the creature.

"I cannot leave you here to limp along this road, miss. Are you going to Tarrington Castle?"

She wanted to deny it, but since she walked along the private drive leading to the castle, the truth seemed obvious. And she couldn't concoct a believable story as to why she would be here otherwise. "I am."

"Then please allow me to assist you. You shouldn't be walking on an injury."

She shivered at the thought of putting herself at the mercy of a horse again. Or the duke. "I can't ride your horse."

"I supposed you could sit crossways, even if it isn't a sidesaddle."

"I can't. I will walk. It isn't far now."

He stopped. She moved more quickly to put some distance between herself and the duke and bit her lip against the pain. Seconds later, the creaking of leather and metal reached her ears. She looked back. He unbuckled the saddle, carried it to the side of the road, and set it down. She turned around to watch. What on earth was he doing?

He went back to the horse, took up the reins, and trotted toward her, leading the horse. As he reached her, he gestured to the horse where only a blanket remained on his back. "You can sit in sidesaddle position on the blanket. He's very steady. He likes ladies; he won't throw you."

To ward him off, she held up her hands. "I'm not riding that horse, not now, not ever." She made no comment on his claim that his horse liked ladies. She didn't want to know how many ladies had ridden his horse nor under what circumstances.

Narrowing his gaze, he bent down a little and peered at her face under her hat. "Aphrodite?"

The blood left her head so quickly that she nearly lost her balance. Her mind emptied of all intelligent thought. "W-what?"

The corners of his mouth lifted. "It is you! Aphrodite. But I suppose it's Miss Palmer. Isn't it?" His smile spreading in triumph, he removed his hat. That shock of blond hair nestling among his ebony waves mocked her.

She let out a frustrated sigh. She should never trust fate to keep her secrets.

"I've been trying to talk to you ever since I found out who you are, but the countess won't let me near you." He rubbed his cheek, and his smile turned rueful. "The Countess of Tarrington is a formidable woman."

Hannah folded her arms and glared. "I can't imagine why my sister wouldn't want you near me."

His smile faded. "You're still angry with me."

"Your powers of observation are truly astounding. Your Grace." She practically snarled his title.

"You have every right to be angry, but please give me another chance. I'm not normally so rash."

"Really," she said dryly.

"Miss Palmer, please, if you knew me at all,

you'd know I normally have excellent control over my impulses."

"How kind of you to lose control at my expense." She shifted her weight onto her good leg.

"I was completely undone. You were so elegant and mysterious and witty." Glancing down, he smiled and brought up his hand filled with a small bouquet. "I brought these for you."

Lilacs. He'd remembered. She squelched her delight at the gesture and made no move to accept them.

His gaze darted over her face. "You are even more beautiful without the mask than I imagined. Younger than I suspected, though." A tiny crease formed in his brow.

She let out an exasperated huff. "Do you recall meeting me before the masque?"

He paused. "Yes, I believe we were introduced a few days ago."

"We have, in fact, met on five separate occasions prior to the ball."

He froze. Blinked. "Five?"

"Yes, indeed. The first time was at a dinner party a year ago. You barely glanced my way, so I'd be surprised if you remembered me. The second time was at your brother's house early this summer. My sister and I came to have tea with Meredith. It was a short visit, and again you barely looked at me. You seemed preoccupied. Or perhaps simply disinterested."

His eyes searched the air as if reading an invisible book in search of memories that matched her words.

"The third time was last month. A group of us had a picnic and picked blackberries. I dropped my basket, and you helped me pick up my spilled berries."

He let out a long exhale and fingered the stems of the lilacs.

She pushed on. "That same afternoon, you bit into a tart and realized it was strawberry. But since you only ate one bite, you suffered a very mild reaction. The fifth was the morning of the ball when you came to visit my brother-in-law. You mistook me for a servant!"

He winced.

"Do you remember any of that? No? Of course not. You only remember the brazen flirt wearing a mask."

"Miss Palmer, in my defense, I seldom pay attention to ladies as young as you. You're what? Fifteen? Sixteen?"

"Eighteen!"

He waved that away. "Nearly half my age. And

if those *very* young ladies I meet are clearly without enough Town polish or confidence to move among the highest circles with the most notoriously judgmental grand dames of society, I make a point not to look at them a second time—especially if they are beautiful because I don't want to tempt myself; I never wish to raise a lady's expectations, and I have a great many duties, so I cannot let myself become distracted by someone I cannot court."

"You were very distracted at the ball, it appears."

He paused, his expression softening. "I certainly was. If I had known who you were, I would not have danced with you a second time, probably not even a first. Nor would I have . . ." He made a circular wave. "You know."

She wouldn't let him off that easily. "Kissed me?"

He winced again. "I apologize if I made you feel unnoticed the previous times we met. I do believe I remember you at the picnic. You were wearing pink, weren't you? I don't think you spoke the entire time."

"No, I'm not normally one for conversation, especially in large groups."

"You certainly spoke at the ball."

"That was easy. I wore a mask, and we were playing a guessing game." Her leg ached in earnest, and dark shadows reached across the road. "I'm going home. My sister will be worried about me." She took another step, but her ankle had stiffened and the pain doubled.

"Please ride my horse." A light of understanding brightened his face. "You're afraid of horses. I remember."

She gritted her teeth and kept limping.

He kept pace with her. "We'll go slowly, and I'll be right here to steady you. You won't fall."

"No," she ground out. She bit her lip to keep from crying out with the pain.

He raised his voice to a stern tone. "Hannah Palmer, I am giving you two choices: either my horse carries you, or I carry you."

At his threat, she pulled out her hatpin, brandishing it like a weapon. "Touch me and I swear I'll . . . I'll put out your eye!"

He paused, sizing her up. With a single, swift motion, he stepped in, grabbed her by the wrist of the hand that wielded the hatpin, and pulled her against his chest. For a few terrifying heartbeats, he held her trapped against him. Every nerve ending blazed with awareness.

He parted his lips, those tempting lips that had taught her a pleasure she'd never dreamed would be so sublime. Instead of kissing her, he said, "Just so you have no delusions that your 'defense' would protect you if I meant you harm."

She stared into his eyes, unable to look away.

He dropped his voice to a whisper and loosened his grip. "But I have no intention of hurting you. Forgive me for speaking to you in such a heavy-handed manner." He released her and stepped back, leaving her off-balance and aching for his touch again.

Clearly only a practiced *roué* had such effect on sensible young ladies like herself. Or maybe she was so hopelessly green that she was prime to fall victim to any smooth charmer—which didn't paint a delightful picture of her future in London. Maybe he was right; she didn't have enough Town polish. The matrons of London would eat her alive, not to mention worldly gentleman who might not have honorable intensions.

He moistened his lips and continued speaking softly. "I cannot leave you to walk injured, especially now that it is growing dark. I know I broke your trust when I kissed you, but I give you my word as a gentleman, I won't take advantage, and I won't let you fall off my horse nor be harmed in any way. Please, *please* allow me to take you home."

Between the burning in her foot and ankle, and the desperate sincerity in his expression, not to mention his achingly handsome face, she relented—probably another lapse in judgment. She and the duke clearly brought out those qualities in each other.

Resigned, she nodded. "Very well."

Mingled relief and satisfaction overcame his features. "Here."

He handed her the lilacs. As he lifted her into his arms, she held her breath. Their bodies pressed together intimately. Though slim, he possessed strength aplenty to hold her without visible effort. That patch of blond hair caught her attention. Was it as soft as it looked? He smelled divine, all male and desirable. His lips caught her fascination. Only inches from hers, they reminded her of how sweetly they'd kissed her.

Her confusing exhilaration from the singular experience of being in the duke's arms changed to fear as they approached the horse. The beast loomed large, an unpredictable creature with big teeth and uncertain temper, likely to spook at anything. Her breath came in ragged gasps. She closed her eyes. The duke carefully sat her upon the blanket on the horse's back with her legs on the horse's left side. She made the mistake of opening her eyes and looking down. The ground fell away at a dizzying distance. The horse shifted his weight underneath Hannah. She turned cold. With the duke's arms still encompassing her, and his head level with her waist, Hannah tried to control her labored breathing. The horse shifted again.

"You're safe," the duke murmured. "Relax."

With one arm still around her, he used his free hand to pet the horse's neck and murmured, "Easy, boy. Be a gentleman."

The horse's ears swiveled back to listen, and he snorted, still prancing.

"She needs your help," continued the duke. "Let's go slowly and take the lady home."

As the horse settled, the duke eyed Hannah. "Good—you're sitting more comfortably now. Let's go. I'll stay right next to you."

Leading the horse, the duke urged the animal to a sedate walk, but Hannah's fear compounded with every step. The horse took several small sideways steps, probably feeling the tension in her body. The duke murmured soothingly, to her or to the horse, she wasn't sure which, but neither of them calmed. She squeezed the lilacs so hard that she crushed several blooms. Perspiration trickled down the side of her face.

With a quick glance at her face, the duke said, "This isn't going to work. I'll have to ride with you."

He led the horse to a stile next to the road. Using the stile as a mounting block in the absence of stirrups, he swung up and settled her in front of him, then reached around her to take the reins. She blushed so hotly she could have caught fire. She was practically sitting across his lap and letting him embrace her. There were just so many things wrong with that. The heat from his chest warmed her left side, and his arms around her created a sensation of safety and danger all at once.

"I won't let you fall," he said. "Trust me."

"I'd probably trust you better if I didn't know you," she said between clenched teeth.

"If you truly knew me, you'd have complete faith in me," he said tightly.

She glanced up at his face. Only inches separated their mouths. "To do what? Compromise me completely?"

Anger rolled over his features, but then he let out a long exhale and composed his face. With his arms around her, he urged the horse forward again. Under the duke's confident command, the horse obediently pranced along the road, his head bobbing.

Finally he said, "I'm sorry. It was ungentlemanly of me. I should have never behaved that way. But I was pretty sure I'd found the perfect lady, and I couldn't think straight."

Pleasure seeped into her. But his "perfect lady" was a role she'd played at a masque, a lady who didn't exist. She was only Hannah, a sickly, shy nobody.

"And I apologize for drawing my blade," he continued. "When that man insulted you, I lost my head. You seem to bring out a side of me I didn't know existed."

Her conscience pricked her, and she softened toward him. "Perhaps it was the mask. I did and said things I don't normally, either."

"Can we start anew?"

She stiffened. "What do you mean?"

He looked wounded. "Nothing nefarious, I promise. Simply begin our acquaintance in a more . . . traditional way."

"We did. I hardly said two words to you, and you instantly forgot my existence."

He flinched. A few seconds passed. He spoke in the same thoughtful tones he'd used as the Musketeer, as Bennett. "The difference was the way you carried yourself. You were confident at the masquerade ball—poised, mature, witty—so I deemed you approachable. Meeting you as the very young and inexperienced sister of the Countess of Tarrington, not to mention how shy you seemed, well, it made you unavailable. So I avoided looking at temptation. It's hard to remember what one doesn't allow oneself to see."

His explanation made sense in a way. After her parents died and she wore black crepe for mourning, she avoided looking at gowns and hats in cheery colors because she couldn't have them while in mourning. Later, she didn't look at them because her family was too poor to afford such finery.

Tarrington Castle came into view, its silvery white spires beckoning in the dimming light like a lighthouse to weary sailors. But it no longer held the appeal she'd expected. Inside the castle, she was alone. Oh, she had Alicia and Cole and their sweet baby, but no family of her own. Bennett's strong arms around her enfolded her in comfort and reassurance. It might be counterfeit to love, but the sensation was hard to ignore. In his arms, her fears about riding the horse had taken a step back—not quite leaving, but at least not leaving her quaking.

Did the duke often hold ladies in such a way? She looked down at the lilacs, a thoughtful gesture, to be sure. But was that only the gesture of a libertine? She might merely have been one in a long line of ladies he'd tried to seduce.

Bennett—the duke, she corrected herself—met her gaze, his features soft and imploring. "Will you forgive me?"

She moistened her lips. "If I ask you a blunt question, will you give me an honest answer?"

He paused. "Very well. You have my word. I owe you complete honesty."

"Do you often kiss ladies?"

His body stiffened. After a moment, he lowered his mouth to her ear and said softly, "No. I don't often kiss ladies, or women of any kind. Despite my behavior toward you, I am not such a scoundrel."

He hadn't been seeking a dishonorable liaison with her. Yet that relief was tempered by the sad truth that he'd kissed Aphrodite, not Hannah Palmer, which meant he'd never kiss her again. Would another man's kiss be so moving? Surely if she found a man she loved, his kiss would eclipse Bennett's. Of course, she still had the London season to survive. And that ugly little fear that she couldn't have children whispered at the futility of dreaming of a family.

The horse snorted and strained against the reins, ratcheting up Hannah's fear, but Bennett held his mount under control. But can one really control a horse—even a man as commanding as the Duke of Suttenberg?

His chest rumbled against her. "You said you loved Shakespeare's comedies. Which is your favorite?"

As she considered his question, her nervousness eased enough for her to sit more comfortably. "Either *Much Ado about Nothing* or *Twelfth Night*."

"What do you like about them?"

"Strong women. In fact, many of his plays have strong women—*The Taming of the Shrew*, for example. Katherine's strength was misplaced at first, but at least she refused to be a doormat."

As they discussed Shakespeare's plays, the trip flew by. Enfolded in his arms, she relaxed against Bennett, soaking in the sensation of being held.

As the sun sank behind the horizon, they arrived at the front door of Tarrington Castle. Then it hit her; she no longer trembled in fear. She'd been so occupied with her conversation with Bennett that her fear had vanished. Amazed, she glanced at him. He'd probably brought up the subject of Shakespeare to keep her mind off her fears. Whether he'd done that out of kindness or necessity, she could not say.

He dismounted and lifted her down. "Can you walk or shall I carry you?"

"I'll walk." She took a cautious step but hissed in her breath.

He swung her into his arms and carried her up the stairs to the front door. Resigned, she put her arms around his neck. She really shouldn't enjoy the safety and well-being that overcame her when he carried her. In fact, she should still be angry with him. But after these past few minutes in his company, she had quite forgiven him. He'd transformed into

Bennett who captured her attention at the masque—considerate, attentive, gentle—not at all the duke who owned the world and viewed everyone as objects to serve him.

Inside, Cole, wearing his overcoat, stood, giving orders to several men who held lanterns. Alicia stood nearby, pale and silent. She turned at Hannah's arrival.

"Hannah!" Alicia rushed forward but stopped short. "You're touching my sister again, Suttenberg."

The men fell silent.

Hannah put up a hand. "It's not what you think. His Grace was kind enough to help me when I twisted my ankle." She smiled in an attempt to lighten the mood. "You know me, my usual clumsy self."

Alicia folded her arms and glared at the duke, obviously unconvinced. Cole dismissed the others and strode toward them, his gaze thunderous.

As Bennett set her down on a nearby chair, he whispered, "You're stronger than you know, just like Katherine. Or Aphrodite." Without waiting for her reply, he stood, facing the others. "I found her limping near the bridge and I could not, in good conscience, allow her to walk so far on an injured foot."

Alicia and Cole wore equally concerned expressions bordering on anger.

She couldn't allow her sister and brother-in-law to believe the worst of Bennett's actions this afternoon. "That's true. I don't know how I would have made it home without his aid."

Alicia glared at the duke but spoke to Hannah. "What did he do, carry you all the way home?"

"No, we rode his horse."

Her sister's amber eyes opened wide. "You rode a horse?"

Hannah nodded. "I didn't think I could do it, but His Grace walked the horse and kept my mind off of it." At Alicia's look of alarm, Hannah rushed on. "We discussed Shakespeare, and I wasn't nearly so afraid."

"Suttenberg?" Cole looked at the duke for verification.

He donned his ducal mien, all traces of her Bennett vanishing. "I give you my word, I did not touch her in an improper way. I admit to a lapse in judgment at the ball, but I hope you know I'd never take advantage of an innocent girl."

Cole let out his breath and dragged a hand through his hair. "Of course. My apologies for doubting your honor. When Hannah didn't come home, we grew anxious. Then you come in carrying her . . ."

"It looked bad," the duke finished.

"Understandable." He bowed to Hannah. "Good evening, Miss Palmer. I hope your ankle heals quickly."

"Thank you for your assistance." She blocked out the memories of his arms around her while they rode and while he carried her to the house. And she most especially blocked out the softness of his kiss at the ball and the stirrings inside her heart.

Alicia crouched in front of Hannah. "Which ankle?"

Hannah lifted her injured foot and held still while Alicia unfastened the boot to examine the damage.

"This changes nothing, I trust?" the duke said. "You're still coming to my hunting lodge in Netherfield in two weeks' time?"

Cole and Alicia exchanged weighted glances. Alicia nodded briefly. Cole's expression relaxed, and he said, "Yes, we're still coming."

The duke smiled. "Excellent. Until then." His gaze rested on Hannah briefly, and her Bennett peeked through his ducal posture. He bowed and strode away, his lean body filling out his suit beautifully. Blushing, Hannah forced her attention back onto her foot.

Alicia stared at her, and her voice took on an incredulous tone. "You like him."

"No!" Hannah put a hand over her eyes. "Oh, I don't know. He was so charming at the ball. And just now, when he brought me home, he was so kind. He took off his saddle so I could ride, and he didn't make me feel foolish for being so afraid. But it's pointless. I'm beneath him."

Alicia sat next to her. "Why do you say that?"

"He's looking for someone who'll be the perfect duchess, not someone young and shy like I am. I'm not mature enough, nor do I have enough Town polish." Not to mention he needed someone to bear children and protect the ducal line. Fate had made her a failure in the most basic feminine duty. She curled her hand into a fist in helpless anger.

"You have plenty of polish," Alicia said indignantly. Then she grew thoughtful. "I admit, being a duchess brings on a great deal of responsibility, not to mention public scrutiny. "Everyone looks to a duchess for comportment, dress, everything. She is usually held as some kind of example to follow, but if she slips up, people are delighted to find evidence she's no better than they. People can be pathetic sycophants to a duchess's face but utterly ruthless behind her back. They do it to a countess, as well." She wrinkled her nose.

Cole broke in. "Suttenberg is always doing everything he should and excelling at it. Naturally, I found it vastly startling, not to mention amusing, to learn he'd lost his head at our ball. It reassured me the rest of us mere mortals aren't as far behind him as it appears."

"You're an earl," Hannah said. "You aren't far behind him in rank."

"Not just rank, but in everything. He seems so perfect. Like my brother Christian." He grimaced but affection softened the expression.

Hannah nodded at the mention of Cole's handsome younger brother. Even Christian fell short in comparison to her Bennett, the Duke of Suttenberg. Intelligent, witty, accepting—even encouraging—of her ideas and dreams, and thoughtful, Bennett truly was as amazing as people thought. He wasn't perfect, but that added to his appeal. Oh heavens, was she losing her heart to him?

Foolish girl! Her feelings were irrelevant. She wasn't meant to be a duchess: she disliked attention, she lacked poise, and most of all loomed that horrifying possibility that she couldn't bear children so crucial to the continuation of the line.

She stared at the lilacs in her hand. "I understand what you're saying; liking him would be pointless."

Alicia touched her arm. "No, not pointless at all, dearest. Your dowry is respectable and being Cole's sister-in-law raises you from the level of a country squire's daughter, and you're so beautiful and kind that everyone admires you. You have no reason to believe yourself beneath consideration. But a duchess is not an easy role to bear."

"I wouldn't want people to watch me and talk about me, nor have false friends." Hannah shook her head. "I won't give him another thought. When we go to his hunting lodge, I will content myself with his library and gardens. The visit will be a pleasant diversion, nothing more."

Alicia hugged her, and they turned their attention to her ankle. Cole carried her up the stairs to her room. Though he was broader and more muscular than the duke, being in his arms invoked none of the pleasure of being in Bennett's. She sighed. She'd have to put thoughts of Bennett out of her head. From now on, he was only the duke.

But that night before she retired, she carefully pressed Bennett's lilacs between the pages of her favorite book.

Chapter Eight

The Duke of Suttenberg stood in the small drawing room of his hunting lodge and tried not to look too often or too longingly at Hannah Palmer. He must resist temptation. Though he'd discovered in her an uncommon delight, someone as young and sweet and inexperienced as she would crumple under the pressures required of a duchess. He wouldn't do that to her. Besides, at thirty, he was nearly twice her age.

She drew his focus. She stood serenely, almost aloof, watching the others with an aura of quiet dignity. While the earl and countess conversed with everyone, Miss Palmer seemed content to observe.

Since the houseguests were all assembled, he began the formal greetings. He led his mother to the Tarringtons. "You remember Lord and Lady Tarrington, of course, Duchess?"

Voices in the room hushed as they often did when he spoke, and the guests turned to watch him.

"Certainly." Mother spoke confidently, unconcerned with the attention.

Lord Tarrington bowed low. "You're looking well, Duchess."

Lady Tarrington curtsied gracefully. "Lovely to see you again, Your Grace."

"Congratulations on the birth of your son," the duchess said.

She received equal looks of pride. "Thank you, Your Grace," Lord Tarrington said. He gestured to Miss Palmer. "Please allow me to introduce Lady Tarrington's sister, Miss Palmer."

With flushed cheeks that only added to her beauty, Miss Palmer curtsied without lifting her gaze.

"My, you are even more beautiful up close," Mother said.

Blushing, Miss Palmer stammered, "Th-thank you. Your Grace."

Suttenberg smiled, hoping to steady her nervousness but she never raised her gaze to his. "I trust your ankle has healed?"

She took her lip between her teeth briefly, those lush, sweet lips he'd kissed once. "Yes, Your Grace. It's . . . well." Her blush turned crimson, and her eyes narrowed as if she were in pain.

Apparently, the question had the opposite effect. Mother looked at her in—was that sympathy or pity?—and moved on to meet the others. Pity was never a good sign. The duchess pitied the unfortunate, not ladies who won her approval. Miss Palmer took a step back and bumped into a small table. It teetered, setting a vase to wobbling. She turned and tried to catch the vase but knocked over a small picture in a frame.

Some of the younger guests giggled. Miss Blackwood, the daughter of a marquis that his mother hoped he'd consider, stared at Miss Palmer as if she were a street urchin.

After throwing a withering glare at the uncharitable girls, Suttenberg went to Miss Palmer's side. He steadied the vase and righted the picture frame. "No harm done," he said.

After darting him a glance, she closed her eyes and swallowed as if trying to prevent tears.

Poor girl. She'd never survive the spotlight always shining on a duchess. Odd, but when she'd pretended to be Aphrodite, she'd been so poised, so confident, not the bashful, clumsy girl he saw now. Even when she'd been limping and frightened of his horse, she hadn't been so awkward.

Miss Palmer's sister, the Countess of Tarrington, went to her and squeezed her hand, giving the girl a sympathetic smile, then straightened her posture as if giving unspoken guidance. Miss Palmer followed suit, but kept her gaze downcast, her cheeks still reddened.

To keep attention off the distraught girl, Suttenberg continued guiding his mother to each guest as if nothing had happened. He greeted Miss Blackwood and her parents without undue warmth, lest they be too encouraged by his attentions, and he welcomed Mr. Gregory, a longtime friend of the family, who managed to show equal parts deference and friendly affection for them both.

Suttenberg clapped Mr. Gregory on the shoulder. "Always glad to see you, Gregory."

"You as well, Your Grace." Mr. Gregory smiled and glanced at the duchess, his smile turning affectionate. "You're radiant, as usual, Duchess."

As Mr. Gregory and Mother exchanged pleasantries, Miss Palmer practically disappeared into the background. After the butler announced dinner, they filed into the dining room and sat at a sumptuous meal, but Bennett hardly tasted it. His focus returned often to Hannah Palmer. She seldom spoke to her dinner companions. Trying to keep to his vow to avoid temptation, and to spare her the guests' focus, he hardly looked at her all evening. Yet she occupied his thoughts all night, even as he tried to sleep.

The following day, after he took all interested guests out to enjoy a morning hunt, he returned home while many of the others went on an extended ride.

Inside the stables, he brushed his hunter, enjoying the uncomplicated pleasure of bonding time with his horse. After he'd finished, he headed for the hunting lodge, absently glancing at the pasture behind the stables where some of the horses grazed. Miss Palmer stood with her arms crossed on top of the fence, her chin resting on them, her attention wholly focused on a pair of colts prancing as if performing a dance for her. Despite his best intentions, he went to her like a moth to the flame. Would he be burned?

He leaned against the fence and watched her, admiring the soft curve of her cheek. His fingers itched to touch it. She continued to stare at the horses in the pasture.

Puzzled by her rapt attention on something that clearly terrified her, he asked, "What is it about horses that frightens you?"

With a little start, she turned to him and smiled ruefully, "Forgive me; I did not see you." She swallowed and returned her focus to the pastures. "I have always been afraid of horses; I feel small and helpless next to such big creatures."

A breeze carried the scents of fallen leaves, apples, and wood smoke. The air currents also teased the curls near her face. He inhaled and took a step closer to her. That aura of serenity that accompanied an unguarded Hannah enfolded him in a loving embrace.

She moistened her lips. "When my brother Armand got a new horse, he wanted so badly for me to ride with him. So he brought out one of the smaller mares and convinced me to try. I had no sooner found my seat when something spooked the horse, and she started running. I was terrified. I was sure I would fall off and die."

"But you didn't."

"No. I stayed on somehow. My brother caught up to us and pulled the horse to a stop. He pulled me off and held me, telling me over and over he was so sorry. I shook all over. I realized then how very little I could control such a big, strong animal. And I don't really understand them. They seem so volatile. They are beautiful, and I love watching them—from a safe distance."

He nodded. "If you understand them, they may not seem so frightening. For example, look." He pointed to a colt with his ears pricked forward. "He's curious. But look at those two at the top of the hill. See the position of their heads? They're aggressive. When they put their heads down and flatten their ears, they're angry. And that one is pawing. He's about to charge. Those by the ridge are relaxed—you can tell by their heads and their postures. That one over there, the little mare, she's listening to us. See how her ears are turned our way?"

Her face brightened. "I see." Her smile turned sheepish. "You know, I'm surprised I haven't noticed that before. I'm normally fairly observant about people. I'm surprised I didn't see that about horses."

"You have to spend time in their company to discern little clues like that."

"Yes, I suppose you're right." She returned her chin to her resting position with her arms atop the fence. "But they're easily spooked. Can that be predicted?"

"Sometimes. Sudden movements or loud noises will often do it. Some horses are more high-strung than others." He turned to study her. "What do you observe about people?"

She began an astonishingly accurate and detailed discourse about each of his guests—their names, habits, and relationships—ending with, "Dr. Power doesn't mind everyone asking him for free medical advice. He's such a gentle, fatherly sort of man. Oh, and Miss Blackwood has set her cap for you, in case you didn't notice."

He nodded. "I did notice."

Miss Blackwood fit all my mother's requirements. From the exterior, she seemed ideal, but she was too calculating. She would not stoop to help a lady who couldn't remember the steps during a dance the way Miss Palmer had. And he could never allow a woman like Miss Blackwood to see the weakness deep inside him, a weakness he feared would reveal itself if he let down his guard.

"But you don't return her regard," Hannah stated.

"I'm not entirely sure she has a heart, and I required that in a wife." He clamped his mouth shut. He seemed to have developed an appalling urge to speak his mind in Hannah's presence.

She smiled as if they were comrades. "I didn't want to say that about her; it would have been impolite. But I agree." Her tone turned wistful. "She probably rides beautifully."

"She does."

"And being the center of attention doesn't fluster her."

"No, I agree; she rather prefers it."

Miss Palmer slumped a little. "I'd never make a good wife for a duke or a lord. I'd be better suited for a country squire—someone who won't seek London society."

He ached to tell her that it didn't matter. With a lady like her at his side, he wouldn't feel so alone, wouldn't feel the need to keep up pretenses every moment of the day, would love to immerse himself in her serenity. But she was right; she'd be happier living the country life with a man who wouldn't subject her to society and London and moments when her shyness would cause her to become flustered and knock over vases, to the delight of gossips.

Her voice drew him from his thoughts. "Mr. Gregory and your mother have a particular fondness for one another."

He chuckled softly. "Oh, no, Mr. Gregory is a longtime friend."

"He doesn't want simple friendship, and I don't believe Duchess does, either."

"Why do you say that?" Suttenberg eyed her.

"They converse like old friends, but every once in a while, they cast longing glances at one another. And once he looked at her with such admiration that I almost teared up. He seems a fine gentleman."

Odd, but Mother had never mentioned Mr. Gregory in that particular way. He'd have to ask her about it later. His mother remarrying? He turned that over in his mind. Honestly, he was surprised she hadn't yet. He'd been five when his father died, and the duchess had been alone ever since. She was still an attractive woman, only in her early fifties, and had a great deal to offer a husband—wit, intelligence, kindness. Certainly she ought to remarry if she had that desire. Suttenberg agreed with Hannah Palmer; Gregory was a fine gentleman.

Miss Palmer's voice broke in to his thoughts. "Your mother is a gracious lady."

He studied her face. "Do you think so?"

"I do. She wasn't condescending at my awkwardness when you presented me to her, nor when I acted like a clumsy fool. She's inordinately fond of you."

He smiled. "She is, fortunately. I hope to stay in her good graces."

"Surely you're not worried. Why, with such a paragon of a son, she must be very proud." She smiled as if enjoying a private joke.

He shook his head. "I'm no paragon, as you well know."

A small chestnut mare trotted to him, nodding her head and nickering a greeting. He smiled affectionately at the old horse. She stretched her neck out over the fence. Miss Palmer stiffened but didn't step away.

"Good morning, Daydream." He rubbed the mare's nose and ran his hands along her neck.

"Are your mother's expectations so high?" Hannah's nonjudgmental compassion as she gazed at him had an odd effect on his tongue.

"I became the Duke of Suttenberg at the age of five."

She nodded and recited, "Bennett Arthur

Partridge, the Fifteenth Duke of Suttenberg." She smiled. "The current book of Peerage is expected reading for any young lady who will have a Season in London." She sobered and touched his sleeve. "What happened then?"

"My mother explained that my rank carried a great deal of responsibility. Not only must I manage my lands, but I must be an example of a peer of the realm to everyone who would watch me. My father had a reputation for excellence, and she wanted me to follow his legacy."

"A heavy load for a five-year-old." She regarded him somberly.

He rested one arm on top of the fence while the other continued rubbing Daydream, who nuzzled him and wuffled in his ear. "She told me the time for catching frogs and learning my letters in the nursery was over. I went to school the next day and spent the rest of my life trying to live up to family ideals."

She covered his hand with hers. Warmth soaked in from the contact all the way to his heart. For a mad instant, he almost tore off their gloves and touched her hand-to-hand. Cheek-to-cheek. Lip-to-lip.

Softly, Hannah asked, "What would happen, do you think, if you failed to live up to that ideal?"

"I'd disappoint her. That alone would be unbearable. And I'd tarnish the family reputation. I'd

119

let down everyone who relies on me to do it right—my younger brother and sister, their children. I'd be a failure."

"Don't you think having weakness is a natural part of being human?"

"I'm a duke. I'm not allowed to have weaknesses."

"Everyone has weaknesses." The softness in her eyes became almost too difficult to bear.

He let out a long, slow breath and revealed one of his greatest fears. "I do have a terrible weakness. My grandfather on my mother's side was Italian—hot-blooded and passionate. He dueled a dozen men, killing over half of them, and had a dozen lovers, leaving illegitimate children scattered over four countries. In the end, his temper proved his undoing. He started a fight, and his opponent killed him. If I let go of my self-control, I'll be just like him—an angry libertine."

She squeezed his hand. "You aren't like that. You won't become that, not even if you let go once in a while."

"I might. Look how I behaved at the ball. I kissed you, someone I'd only just met, and I drew a sword."

"Well, then, clearly the answer is to avoid masques. And pirates." A teasing light entered her soft brown eyes.

He shook his head, uncomfortably aware of how much he'd confided in this sweet girl. "Most of my friends don't know anything I told you."

"Do you have the wrong friends, then? Or do you have an aversion to allowing them to see the real man inside?"

He hesitated. "I'm not certain."

"I'll keep your confidence," she said gravely.

He gazed at the lovely lady next to him. How could he could have been so foolish as to have overlooked her before? At first he'd been blinded by his quick assessment that she was too young and shy and awkward. He'd almost missed the joy of knowing her, of knowing what it was like to reveal his true self to someone. Hannah Palmer was artless, with no hidden agenda, no practiced flirtatiousness, no carefully cultivated games.

She allowed him to be his true self in her presence. He hadn't spoken to anyone with such candor in longer than he could remember. The idea of spending all his days with such an enchanting, genuine lady left him almost desperate with longing.

Daydream bumped Hannah with her nose. The girl jerked back.

"She won't hurt you," Suttenberg said soothingly. "This is Daydream. She's very gentle." He held out a hand to Hannah. "Come meet her. She's the first horse I learned to ride."

After a brief hesitation, Hannah placed her hand in his and let him lead her back to the fence. Her trust in him made him want to puff out his chest. He put Hanna's palm under Daydream's nose to get her scent. After the chestnut snuffled, Suttenberg put Hannah's small hand on the horse's neck and guided her to stroke it.

"Look at her ears," he murmured. "And see how she holds so still? She likes you."

Hannah's mouth curved in a tentative smile. "I want to touch her." She removed her glove and put her bare hand on the horse's neck.

"She's softest right between the nostrils." He petted the area to demonstrate.

Hannah followed his lead, her lips curving upward in delight. "She's just like velvet."

They stood side by side, petting a horse as if it were the most natural thing in the world. He'd never felt so comfortable with a lady before—comfortable except for a growing longing to draw her into his arms.

If only he could keep her at his side and hold on to the relaxed, easy joy of having her near. A few loose curls slipped from her hat and framed her face. She glanced up at him with an almost teasing smile. The image of Aphrodite superimposed itself over her. Aching, burning to touch her, he traced a finger down her cheek.

"You're unlike anyone I've ever met," he murmured.

Warmth and affection shone in her eyes. No moment in his entire life had been as perfect as this. No lady had ever been so perfectly suited for him, the real him, Bennett. He cupped her face with his hands, leaned in, and kissed her. The softness of her lips took his breath away. She kissed him back, with more heat than before, and he slipped into a sweet bliss he only experienced with her.

"Marry me," he whispered as he broke the kiss. "I need you. I want you."

She stared, her mouth working silently, then said, "I thought we agreed I'm not suited for the role of a duchess—certainly not the Duchess of Suttenberg."

He pulled her in against his chest, savoring the softness of her body and the way it molded against his. "I don't care. I don't care if you can't ride and don't like large gatherings and get flustered when everyone watches you. I need you for quiet moments like this, when I can be who I really am and tell you my thoughts. When I'm with you, I forget I'm the Duke of Suttenberg, and I become just Bennett."

She pulled away enough to look into his eyes, and put a hand on his cheek, the same cheek she'd slapped after their last kiss. "You'd soon regret marrying me—your mother would disapprove, I'd embarrass you in public, I'd fail you in some crucial way. Something will happen, or fail to happen, and you'll wish you'd married someone more like Miss Blackwood—with a heart, of course." She raised up and kissed him softly. "Thank you for the offer, but I must decline."

He tightened his hold on her. "Don't. Please don't."

"Perhaps we oughtn't spend time together alone." Regret dimmed the light in her brown eyes. She stepped out of his arms and walked away.

Pain pierced his heart. His hot blood screamed at him to run after her, to do whatever he must to secure her in his life.

Control. Maintain control. He fisted his hands and turned away. He must accept her logic. She wasn't suited for London life and all that would be required of her as a duchess. His duty came above his own need—the need for a wife he could love, a wife who would love him for who he was.

He hung his head and almost gave in to the urge to weep.

Chapter Nine

Hannah sat in her bedroom with her fingers to her lips, reliving the glorious kiss of Bennett Arthur Partridge, the Fifteenth Duke of Suttenberg, and made no attempt to suppress the tears streaming down her face.

Bennett. He wanted her to love him for the man, not the duke. And heaven help her, she did love him. His proposal seemed so sincere, as had his kiss. She'd almost accepted. The idea of sharing her life with a man of such strength and gentleness, of sophisticated polish and the type of kindness that he removed a saddle to let her ride his horse, who confided his private fears, who kissed her like she was the most important and loved woman in his life, left her breathless with wonder. Oh, she yearned to accept.

His proposal had probably been another momentary lapse, like those that had driven his actions at the ball. If she'd accepted, he, as a man of honor, would have followed through and married her. But he'd grow to regret it. And he'd resent her when she failed him at every turn. Not only would she be the duchess everyone would ridicule, which would shame him and his family, but she'd fail him as a wife in her most basic role, that of bearing a future duke. He needed an heir; to deny him that would be unthinkable. The sorrowing suspicion that had plagued her for years sharpened into true pain now that it was Bennett's children she wanted. The harsh truth glared at her.

She lay down on the window seat and gave in to her grief. After a time, her tears dried. She stared at the trees swaying in the autumn wind, casting off their gold and crimson leaves, as if casting off hope for life.

Alicia came in, carrying the train of her riding habit over her left arm. "How was your morning? Did you enjoy your walk?"

Hannah pushed herself up to a seated position and hoped her sister wouldn't detect her sorrow. "It was . . . pleasant."

Alicia sat next to her, her cheeks wind-kissed pink. "I'm so glad to hear it." She let out a happy sigh. "It was a lovely day to ride. The men caught several pheasants for dinner, so we'll eat well tonight."

Hannah tried to muster some enthusiasm. "I haven't have pheasant in ages."

Her performance didn't convince her sister. "Do you have another headache? You know, you should consult Dr. Power. He's a sought-after physician in London."

"No, I'm well." Hannah drew in her knees and hugged them.

"What then?"

Hanna rested her chin on her knees. "I don't think I should go to London."

"Because you bumped into a table last night under the duchess's scrutiny?" Alicia touched her back.

"Not only that. I just . . . I don't think the kind of gentleman who'd want to marry me will be there."

"Where do you think he'll be?"

"Living in a small estate in the country."

Alicia put an arm around her. "Oh, my dear, you have much to offer any gentleman. Don't make assumptions about them; you'll be wrong most of the time." She smiled wryly, probably remembering all the assumptions she'd made about Cole. "Give it a month. If you hate London, we'll go home and see about finding you a poor country squire."

Of course, Hannah's failure to produce heirs might disappoint even a poor country squire, but at least the fate of a duchy wouldn't be at stake. And she couldn't bear such disappointment in Bennett's eyes. She almost let out a moan. She must not think of him as Bennett; he must be His Grace or the duke forevermore.

"As you wish." She glanced at Alicia, too weary to continue this conversation with her emotions so raw. "I think I feel a headache coming on. Perhaps I shall take a nap."

Alicia stood. "I'll let you rest." She closed the door quietly behind her. But a few minutes later, Alicia returned. "I hope you don't mind, but I asked Dr. Power to look in on you. He's here, with your permission."

Oh dear, caught in her lie. But if he was a sought-after London doctor . . .

"Very well. Send him in." Hannah stood.

Alicia gave her a sympathetic smile and left them alone.

The silver-haired Dr. Power entered. "Miss Palmer? I understand you are suffering from a headache?"

"I'm better now. But . . ."

He passed an assessing glance over her. "Can I do anything for you?"

"Doctor, may I ask you a question?"

"Of course." The kindly gentleman took a few steps nearer.

She let out her breath, shaking all over. If a

renowned doctor confirmed her fears, it would cement them forever. And if she knew ahead of time that she couldn't have children, she should not, in good conscience, marry anyone, unless perhaps to a widower who already had them. Perhaps the doctor knew of a treatment or a way she could still bear a child.

The idea of sharing her life or having children with anyone but Bennett left her empty.

The doctor adjusted his spectacles. "Anything you tell me will be kept in strictest confidentiality."

She nodded, clasping and unclasping her hands, and drew a shaking breath. "I wondered if you have much experience with women who get headaches so strong that light and noise becomes intolerable and often last all day, sometimes longer."

"Yes, I have a few patients who suffer from that malady."

She hesitated, afraid to ask the question; afraid of its answer. "I was sickly as a child, and while I'm healthier now, I still have those kinds of headaches. And I wondered, are they symptoms of something worse? Something that make it difficult for a woman to bear a child?"

He gestured for her to sit and took a seat next to her. He gave her a fatherly smile. "No, miss. I know of no correlation between the sick headache and the ability to procreate."

She held her breath. "Truly?"

"I vow it."

She pressed a hand to her chest, hardly daring to believe it. The dark fear she'd borne for years dissipated, but didn't entirely vanish. It seemed too perfect to be real.

As if sensing she needed further proof, he added, "All of my patients—both men and women—who suffer from the sick headache, also known as migraines, have many sons and daughters. There is no reason to believe you won't, when the time comes."

She searched his face. A respected London doctor surely knew what he was about. And she'd observed his confidence and sincerity over the course of their visit. As the reality of his assurance sank in, she almost sobbed in relief. She might still be a green, unpolished girl who suffered from shyness and awkwardness, but at least she might know the joys of motherhood. If she ever married.

He smiled kindly. "Have you carried that fear all your life?"

She nodded.

"There are many reasons why women cannot conceive or deliver healthy babies—some reasons we may never understand except that it is God's will—but your headaches should not preclude you from bearing children."

"Thank you. I'm so relieved." Tears welled up in her eyes as the last of her fears vanished.

"I'm happy to have provided some comfort to you." He patted her hand and left.

Hugging herself, Hannah leaned her head against the window. She might be a mother someday. A weight lifted from her soul.

But her ability to produce heirs didn't make her capable of fulfilling the role of a duchess with all its responsibilities and pressures—not to mention being married to a paragon of charm and elegance, whom everyone would think had settled for an awkward little mouse.

Perhaps someday she'd find another man who would kiss her the way Bennett had and who would help her stop dreaming about the man she could never have. She didn't know whether to laugh or cry at the absurd thought.

Chapter Ten

Trying to forget the sweet girl who'd stolen his heart, Suttenberg threw himself into his duties, meeting with his steward, hosting his guests, hunting, fencing, and providing entertainment—all while trying to avoid Hannah without making it appear as if he was doing so. His efforts mocked him as meaningless.

On the last night of the house party, Suttenberg sat next to his mother. With a little luck, his guests would view his mood as stylishly aloof instead of wounded. How would he ever find a lady who would take Hannah Palmer's place in his heart? He'd never believed love would happen so quickly, nor take such hold of him.

Against his will, he glanced at her—so lovely and untouchable that it almost hurt to look at her. She sat amid a small group of guests, watching them with that assessing way of hers, giving almost no input unless questioned. When someone did bring her into the conversation, her answers sometimes brought laughter and some brought pensiveness. Mostly she remained quiet, content to observe. Miss Blackwood eyed her with cold disdain, but Hannah appeared to give no notice except for glances akin to amusement.

The duchess leaned over and spoke in his ear. "You're right, Suttenberg. Miss Blackwood would be a perfect duchess, except the primary emotion she possesses is contempt." She paused. "Pity Miss Palmer is so shy. Not only is she uncommonly lovely, she's intriguing and has a depth one misses at first glance.

He nodded, not trusting himself to speak. Remembering his vow to pay more attention to the gentleman that Hannah Palmer suggested had captured his mother's affection, he looked about the room for Mr. Gregory. Their longtime friend, a gentleman with a modest estate, glanced at Mother, a soft smile flitting over his features. Mother smiled back and let out an almost imperceptible sigh.

Suttenberg eyed his mother. "Mother, may I ask an impertinent question?"

"Certainly."

"Why is it that you never remarried?"

"Oh, well, you know . . ." She waved a hand.

"No, I don't know. Tell me."

She studied her fingers, looking almost wistful. "I am the Duchess of Suttenberg. I cannot marry just anyone."

"Why? You've been alone a long time. I have the estate well in hand. You have a generous jointure. Why couldn't you follow your heart?"

"It wouldn't be right if I were to marry too far below my station."

"I can't imagine why not. Who would dare gainsay you?"

"Oh, people would whisper. And any good man would know not to reach too high."

"Any good man would follow his heart." As the words left his mouth, he gave a start. If he hadn't heard himself utter it, he would never have believed he'd made such a statement. As he turned it over in his mind, it rang true. Whether it was a secret belief he'd only now acknowledged or a profound change in his principles, he couldn't say.

His mother stared at him in wonder. "You are the last person I would have expected to hear speak those words."

He let out an uneasy laugh and tried to shrug. "If he's respectable and would treat you well, then he's surely not beneath you."

She said nothing for a while. Finally, she turned tortured eyes upon him. "I have found someone but you wouldn't approve and I can't disappoint you."

Aghast, he stared. He lowered his voice. "You are in love with someone, but you haven't married him because I wouldn't think he's good enough?"

She flicked an imaginary speck off her gown. "I know all too well how important image is to this family. To you."

"Hang the family image. Do you love him?"

She let out a sigh. "Yes."

"Does he love you?"

She glanced at Mr. Gregory, who caught her gaze. His features turned to alarm as if he suspected they discussed something that distressed her. "Yes, I believe he does."

Suttenberg stood and offered a hand to her. "Come with me, please." They crossed the room to Mr. Gregory. "Sir, please join me in the conservatory."

Mr. Gregory paled and glanced anxiously at the duchess. "Of course, Your Grace."

Unbelievable that a man who had known Suttenberg since he was an infant addressed him with such deference. Was he so pompous and untouchable that he drove everyone away, including suitors of his sister and mother?

He led them to the conservatory. "Close the door, Gregory, if you please."

The gentleman did so, looking as if he were about to be tied to a post and lashed.

Suttenberg eyed him. "Your estate is small but fairly prosperous, is it not?"

Gregory blinked. "Yes, Your Grace. You yourself have helped me with crop techniques. My tenants are hardworking, and we turn a modest profit every year."

"So, you aren't destitute?"

"No, Your Grace."

"Has anyone ever accused you of being a fortune hunter?"

Mr. Gregory stepped back in surprise. "No, Your Grace."

"And you aren't a rake? You don't gamble or drink excessively or trifle with women?" He knew the answers to this line of questioning, of course, but wanted them to see he was being thorough.

Gregory looked more horrified with every question. "Oh, no, Your Grace."

Suttenberg paced across the floor amid a plethora of tropical plants, enjoying himself but trying to look grim and thoughtful. "So, you have much to offer a wife?"

"I . . ." Gregory trailed off. "I think so, but that depends on the lady."

Suttenberg nodded. "I understand that you have formed an attachment for the duchess."

After another glance at Mother, Mr. Gregory drew himself up and spoke to them both. "Yes, Your Grace. I have loved the duchess for years."

"Did you declare yourself?"

He hung his head. "As much as I want to, no. I would be reaching too far above me."

Suttenberg turned to his mother. "Do you love him?"

"Yes," Mother almost sobbed.

"Do you care about his rank or his wealth—or the lack thereof?"

"No."

"Would you marry him if he asked you—if I gave my blessing?"

She looked like a child about to reach for a longed-for gift. "Yes."

"Then for heaven's sakes, Gregory, you have my blessing. Will you two just get married and stop mooning over each other?"

Mr. Gregory and the duchess ran into each other's arms. Suttenberg turned away to give them privacy.

The duchess's voice stopped him. "Bennett."

He froze. She hadn't called him by his Christian name in years.

She gave him a dazzling smile. "Perhaps you ought to take your own advice, son. If love is good enough for me, it's good enough for you, as well."

He paused with his brows raised.

She nodded toward the door. "I believe there is

a lovely girl in the other room, perhaps without all the qualities one would expect from a duchess, but with many qualities desirable in a wife—a girl you can't seem to keep your eyes off of." She smiled as she rested her head on Gregory's shoulder.

Suttenberg didn't need to be told twice. He made no comment as he left the conservatory. He shouldn't be surprised Mother had noticed his preference for Hannah Palmer, despite his attempts to keep his feelings hidden. She was right; Hannah might not be as cool and poised as some believed a duchess must be, but she was in possession of every character trait he most admired. And he loved her. He should take his own advice.

He sought out Lord and Lady Tarrington, inviting them to join him in the library. They eyed him curiously as he paced. "I have a problem. I have fallen in love with Hannah. I asked her to marry me yesterday—I hope you will forgive me for not seeking your permission first—but she refused. She said she's not the kind of person who would make a good duchess. But I cannot let her go. And I believe she has feelings for me, as well."

Tarrington grinned. "Permission granted. But she must willingly agree to marry you; I won't coerce her."

"Nor would I want you to, of course. Lady Tarrington?"

She narrowed her gaze. "You kissed her again, didn't you?"

He gulped. "I did. I can't seem to control myself around her. She is the most wonderful, remarkable, genuine lady I have ever met, and I am quite hopelessly in love with her."

The Countess of Tarrington stepped forward and raised her hand.

He tensed.

She patted his cheek and smiled. "Then go and woo her—gently."

He almost shouted his happiness. After giving instructions to the nearest servants, he practically raced to the drawing room where the other guests gathered. "Ladies and gentlemen, I suggest we dance. Miss Blackwood, since you are such an accomplished pianist, will you play for us? Begin with a waltz, if you please."

Without any expression, even surprise at the request for a waltz at the beginning of the evening, the cold beauty stood and went immediately to the piano. The gentlemen helped servants push furniture to the edges of the room and roll up the carpets to transform the drawing room into a small ballroom.

Suttenberg went to Hannah and held out a hand. "Dance with me, my Aphrodite, I beg you."

She blinked, and a slow smile curved her

delicious lips. Her chin lifted, and her posture straightened. "I'm not certain I ought to dance with a mere mortal such as you at two different balls."

"Then I thank you from the bottom of my heart that you have deemed me worthy of your divine presence once again."

As he took her in dance position, his body sighed as if finding its missing parts. She slipped completely into the goddess role and moved with him with all of his Aphrodite's grace and poise.

While he spun her around the room, contentment and joy wrapped around him. "You know, a goddess could easily play the role of duchess."

Her façade slipped but returned in a thrice. "A goddess does whatever she wants. A duchess has to obey society laws and have large parties and ride horses."

"A duchess doesn't have to do anything. Most view her as almost a goddess."

"She's expected to follow certain conventions. A duke needs a duchess who will."

"Not this duke."

Her eyes widened, but he said nothing further. Instead, he kept conversation on lighter matters, flirting with her as he had at the masque and enjoying her flirting in return.

As the dance ended and they bowed and

curtsied, he took her hand. "Take a turn about the gardens with me?"

She went still, considering.

He held his breath. If she refused, he'd try again and again. He would not lose her.

Chapter Eleven

Hannah paused. Did she dare go outside alone with Bennett? He had a habit of kissing her when they were alone, unless she was limping.

She glanced at her sister, who smiled so broadly at her that a light seemed to come from her. "You appear to have won over my sister," Hannah said.

"At least she didn't slap me this time. I'll have to tread more lightly around your family—very strong women. Katherine would be proud."

She smiled at the reference to the Shakespearean characters they'd discussed when they'd ridden his stallion. She could apologize for her sister's conduct, but apologizing for the actions of a countess seemed presumptuous. Besides, at the time he'd deserved it. She settled for giving him a saucy grin that would have pleased Aphrodite.

As Bennett led her outside, Hannah inhaled the chill, earthy air. A bright autumn moon bathed the gardens in a soft glow. Their feet crunched in a carpet of fallen leaves. The pale patch in his hair seemed to glow in the semidarkness.

Chill bumps peppered her arms. "Perhaps I should have gotten a shawl."

He took off his coat and draped it around her shoulders. "Don't go in just yet, please."

She cocked her head, as daring as she'd been on the night of the masque. "Are you going to kiss me again?"

"Most certainly. First, I must tell you something." He moistened his lips. Something vulnerable entered his expression. "I love you."

Her breath stilled. He loved her? Despite all her shortcomings?

He took both of her hands in his. "I want you at my side wherever I go. I want to show you my estates and introduce you to my tenants. I want to show you what London has to offer and take you to the seashore where we'll swim together. I want to tell you what I'm thinking and feeling, knowing I can trust you to accept me as I am, a human with fears and weaknesses. I want to hold you in my arms at night and wake up next to you in the morning. I want you to always be honest with me and tell me what you think." He drew her closer, gently, as if giving her a chance to step away if she desired. But into his arms is where she longed to go.

She opened her mouth to speak, but he put a finger over her lips. "I want to get old with you. I don't care for parties and balls; those aren't required to serve in Parliament. And on the occasions we do attend a gathering, if you remain as quiet as you wish, everyone will think you're mysterious."

She latched on to the sentiment her sister had expressed once. Perhaps they were both right.

With his fingers still over her lips, Bennett continued, "If you only choose to surround yourself with your closest friends, people will think you are discerning. If you only have small parties, society will view them as exclusive. When you find yourself obligated to enter society, bow to the queen, and so forth, all you need to do is pretend to put on your Aphrodite mask and you'll be perfect. The rest of the time, be your genuine self. I love you as you are."

He loved her. He truly loved her! And he had given such carefully worded, wise counsel that she actually dared believe him. The instant he called her Aphrodite before they'd danced, she had automatically fallen into the poise she'd adopted at the ball while in costume. That proved she could do it at will. Now that an expert had assured her that she had no reason to fear that she'd fail to produce an heir, her greatest fear of all, her other concerns faded away as too meaningless to consider.

"Please, Hannah, please marry me. I promise I'll live every day trying to make you happy."

A little ripple of pleasure ran over her skin at the sound of her given name uttered in his voice. She kissed his finger still over her lips. He removed the finger and offered a sheepish smile, but intensity, almost desperation, darkened his eyes.

Stepping nearer, she placed a hand on his chest. His heart thumped against her palm. "Before I give you my answer, I want you to promise me something."

"Anything." He ripped off his gloves and touched her face, running his fingers up and down her cheeks, a pleasantly distracting motion.

She touched that blond patch of hair that contrasted so sharply with his dark waves. It was, indeed soft, but no softer than the rest of his hair. "Promise me you will only wear your mask of the paragon in public, and when you're alone with me, you will be simply Bennet."

He awarded her the most glorious smile she'd ever seen. "You are the only one with whom I trust to be myself, and if you call me Bennett, I will have no trouble remembering."

"Then I shall, Bennett. If you can be the real you in my presence, I can be Aphrodite in public as your wife."

"As my duchess."

She smiled, no longer terrified at the thought. "As your duchess."

He wrapped his arms around her and kissed her. The explosion of warmth and pleasure nearly took her breath away.

The love, the sheer passion, pouring into her through his kiss transported her to a world of joy and beauty she'd never dared dream. Every inch of her body sighed as the missing piece to the puzzle of her life fitted into place. All her life had led to this single, glorious, perfect moment. And she belonged there. With him.

Chapter Twelve

Hannah smiled at her husband as he escorted her into the ballroom at Tarrington Castle. Though this year the Countess of Tarrington's ball was not a masque as last year's had been, Hannah firmly wore her Aphrodite persona as if she were in costume. When she entered a room on the arm of the Duke of Suttenberg, such a feat came easy now.

He glanced at her, the corners of his lips curving and his eyes shining with adoration. "You look beautiful, my goddess."

"You are handsome as ever, my delicious mortal," she purred.

Abandoning his usual reserve, he broke into a broad grin. A moment later, and Bennet transformed back into the Duke of Suttenberg.

All eyes fixed on them, and murmurs of what a handsome couple they were, and how mysterious the duchess was, rippled around the room. Hannah only smiled. They were, indeed, a handsome couple, and she'd grown comfortable smiling mysteriously when she could think of nothing to say. As the Duchess of

Suttenberg, she'd managed not to embarrass herself or her husband during the London Season. She'd even bowed to the queen and backed away wearing a hoopskirt and train without tripping. And, if her suspicions were correct, she now carried Bennett's child. How different she was from the girl she'd been a year ago.

Alicia and Cole greeted them. Hannah hugged her sister, whom she now outranked—a thought that always made her shake her head at the ironies of fate. As she caught the glances of familiar faces, she nodded. Fortunately, she'd built a reputation for saying little.

As the duke paused to speak with someone, Mr. Hill approached. "Good evening, Duchess."

She turned her head slowly and said with cool reserve, "Mr. Hill."

"I—" He glanced at the duke. "I just wanted to congratulate you. I wish you all the best." He smiled tentatively.

"Thank you, Mr. Hill."

After casting another furtive glance at the duke, Mr. Hill bowed and backed away. Nearby, the Buchanan twins flirted with young ladies barely out of the schoolroom.

The musicians struck up the dance introduction, and Cole and Alicia headed up the line. The duke led

Hannah to stand next to them. Others lined up behind them. As the dance began, Hannah smiled at her husband, admiring the grace with which he moved, the beauty of his face, the signature blond shock of hair surrounded by dark waves. Sometimes she still could hardly believe he was hers.

As the set ended, he grinned mischievously at her. She knew that grin. Trying to keep a silly smile off her face, she went with him into the library. Bennett tugged her into his arms and kissed her so thoroughly she wasn't sure she could continue standing.

After he ended the kiss, he chuckled. "I couldn't help myself. You looked so tempting, I just couldn't resist."

"How very fortunate for me." She put a hand on either side of his face and caressed his cheeks. "And now, allow me not to resist."

She kissed him until he groaned. "Aphrodite, you must leave off or I won't be able to go back into that room full of people. I am only a mortal, after all. There is a limit to my endurance."

"I'm counting on that," she said huskily.

They cast off their masks of the duke and the goddess and spent a few minutes together as just Bennett and Hannah, the happiest people at the Autumn Ball.

About Donna Hatch

Donna Hatch is the award-winning author of the best-selling "Rogue Hearts Series." She discovered her writing passion at the tender age of 8 and has been listening to those voices ever since. A sought-after workshop presenter, she juggles her day job, freelance editing, multiple volunteer positions, not to mention her six children (seven, counting her husband), and still manages to make time to write. Yes, writing IS an obsession. A native of Arizona, she and her husband of over twenty years are living proof that there really is a happily ever after.

For other books by this author, or for more information and to take place in contests, giveaways, and behind-the-scenes sneak peeks, visit:

Website: www.donnahatch.com
Blog: www.donnahatch.com/blog
Connect on Facebook: www.facebook.com/RomanceAuthorDonnaHatch
Follow on Twitter: https://twitter.com/donnahatch

If you like this story, please help spread the word and rate or review it on Amazon, Goodreads, and other book review sites.

Thank you!

Made in the USA
Middletown, DE
05 May 2022

65340538R00088